The Blacksmith's Unwelcome Winter Bride

Cheryl Wright

Copyright

THE BLACKSMITH'S UNWELCOME WINTER BRIDE
(Unwelcome Brides Series – Book Eight)

Copyright ©2025 by Cheryl Wright

Small Town Romance Publications

Dedication

To Margaret Tanner, my very dear friend and fellow author, for her enduring encouragement and friendship.

To Alan, my husband of over fifty years, who has been a relentless supporter of my writing and dreams for many years.

To You, my wonderful readers, who encourage me to continue writing these stories. It is such a joy knowing so many of you enjoy reading my stories as much as I love writing them for you.

Table of Contents

Chapter One

Plainville, Montana – 1880s

The only daughter of a respected pillar of the community, Peggy Martin, had always known her father as a good man.

She was still reeling from his recent and unexpected death. Why anyone would murder William Martin, she had no idea. For as long as she could remember, Father had been nothing but kind and caring. His work at the local hospital was a testament to his life's work.

"We know you're in there." A cold, hard voice clearly echoed inside the cottage. "Either open the door or we'll break it down."

Peggy was confused. And scared. It was incomprehensible why someone was attempting to forcibly enter the cottage, her only place of tranquility since Father's death. Moving soundlessly to the window, she pulled back the curtain, hoping the slight movement was not visible from the outside.

What she saw shocked Peggy.

Two men, tall and solid, stood at the door, their hands hovering above their holsters. With no means to defend herself, the only option left for Peggy was to flee. Her mind in a muddle, Peggy couldn't think straight. Should she grab some of her possessions, or just go?

The thought brought her to a halt. What had her father said? If he should die unexpectedly, there was something she had to locate, then flee. At the time, she'd believe it to be a joke, except he wasn't laughing.

Now, it seemed, her life was in jeopardy.

"I'm losing patience, Miss Martin," the cold voice threatened as he pounded on the door. "Margaret," he said, trying to appear more friendly. Except no one called her Margaret, which meant they didn't know her. More likely than not, they barely knew her father.

Were these men hired killers? It was clear they were responsible for her father's death. Her heart thudded.

Peggy sat restlessly on the side of her father's bed, her mind jumbled. Not only from the threat standing outside the cottage door but trying to remember what it was Father had told her. Peggy's eyes filled with tears. She was not a crier. She never had been, but a mere two days after her father's murder, and a day after his funeral, two men menacing her was more than she could bear.

She rifled through her father's desk and found nothing of interest. Moving quickly, she opened the drawer of his robe, and noticed an item wrapped in one of her father's shirts. What she found was a small tin containing letters her mother had written. This couldn't be what those men were after. Could it?

Peggy sighed. The thumping on the door became louder by the minute. She had always believed living on the outskirts of town was a good thing. Now she understood in times like this, it was the complete opposite. She continued to search, not finding anything.

As a last resort, she opened her father's closet. Few clothes hung in there, and those that did, were hanging at a strange angle. She couldn't understand why.

Peggy gazed at the inside of the robe, then studied the outside. The depth outside was larger. It didn't make sense. She put it down to her muddled mind.

As the pounding became even louder, Peggy knew a decision had to be made. She pushed at the back of the closet. It moved a little, but not enough. At the risk of harming herself, she kicked the wood panel until it gave way.

Staring in disbelief, Peggy found a metal box she had never seen in her entire life.

Was this what those men were after? Peggy carefully opened the lid, terrified of what she might find. Her first thought was a gun, although she'd never known William Martin to possess a firearm of any kind.

Instead, she found a journal. Peggy opened it with trepidation. She was met with a combination of a journal and a ledger. Accompanied by a roll of banknotes. Her eyes scanned some of the pages. This ledger had to be what those awful men were after. It made Peggy feel ill and lightheaded to think her father had been involved in something like this.

In a split second, she knew there was no choice but to run, and take the ledger with her. Peggy had no other thought but to get away. Otherwise, she would be collateral damage, just like her father had been.

She shoved the journal down the front of her gown, then hurriedly moved into her own bedroom. There, Peggy snatched up her reticule, along with a thick coat. It was then she heard the crashing of the front door.

She hurried into the bathroom, opening the trap door her father had installed many years ago. The mat he secured to the trap door covered its existent.

Peggy finally understood his reason for installing it. She dreaded climbing in under the cottage, which she knew to be full of spiders and other creepy crawlies, but it was that or lose her life.

She quietly lifted the mat, pulling the door open in the process, then climbed into the last place in the world she wanted to be. She silently closed the trapdoor leaving no trace of her escape route.

Her only hope was to sneak away while those terrifying men searched the cottage looking for her and the journal. Peggy prayed they had no other accomplices who might find her.

As if in a daze, Peggy found herself waiting at the stagecoach depot. She bought a ticket using a false name. To where, she had no idea. Nor did she care. The stagecoach was due any moment, and her heart pounded as she waited for it to arrive.

Glancing around, Peggy was convinced she was safe. For now at least. She noticed dust in the distance, and hoped safety was only minutes away. She had no clothes, except for those on her back, and her only possession was her reticule. She'd taken the roll of notes. Surely Father had left them there to ensure their safe escape?

Her biggest fear was those men finding her before she was safely hidden on the stagecoach. Most likely they knew what she looked like, but she had no idea who to look for. One of the men spoke, and that was her only clue to their identity.

Peggy felt lightheaded. She was certain it was born of panic, and she tried to quell her fears. Unfortunately, it wasn't working. The only way she would feel better was to be installed on the stagecoach and be driven away from here as quickly as possible.

Already having second thoughts about the trip, but also knowing she had little choice, Peggy watched the stagecoach slow down. Dust flew up and hit her in the face. She rubbed at her eyes, trying to clear the debris.

When she glanced up again, the stagecoach had come to a complete halt. She watched as the passengers alighted, then quickly took her place inside the now empty coach. She slouched down as much as possible without getting down on the floor. Not knowing what those men looked like put her at a huge disadvantage.

"Ma'am," a male voice said, and her head shot up. He gazed at her strangely, and Peggy knew what he was thinking – that she was a runaway. Except at her age, it would be comical. "Do you have luggage?" he asked gently.

"I…" her voice faltered. Instead, she shook her head.

She was still alone in the stagecoach, which suited Peggy fine. "Is there anything I can do to help, Ma'am," he asked, as though he understood her situation. When she didn't answer, he moved closer. "Is your life in danger?" he whispered this time.

Peggy nodded, her heart pounding. She wasn't sure she could trust this man, but he seemed to care. "You are the only passenger, Miss Straughn," he said. His expression revealed his thoughts – he knew it wasn't her real name. "We can leave immediately."

He then closed the door, pulling down the leather coverings. Peggy wasn't certain if that was to keep the dust away or hide her from view. Her first instinct was the latter. This man seemed to have her safety at the front of his mind.

It was what Peggy needed, and she nodded, not trusting herself to speak. Moments later, they began to move, and they were on their way to goodness knew where.

Chapter Two

Granville, Montana

Lyle Peterson wiped the sweat from his brow. Being a blacksmith was fiery work, but someone had to do it. Besides, he'd trained for this since he was old enough to swing a hammer. It had always been his father's plan that Lyle take over his blacksmith business. It wasn't a job you continued into old age.

He was almost finished the wheel repair when he heard it. The noise was akin to the sound of a bullet racing past. Except it was far louder, and the sound was not far behind him. Taking care not to burn himself, Lyle spun around.

There was nothing visible to cause the disruption to his work. Perplexed, he turned back to finish the wagon wheel. The unfortunate owner of the wheel would be arriving in the next hour or two.

As he plunged the wheel into cold water, he again heard an unusual sound. This time it was different. "Who's there?" he called out but received no response. Still invested in the wheel, he finished his work, curious as to what he'd heard.

Intriguing as it was, Lyle was convinced someone, or something, was here in the blacksmith's shop. Until he was free to do a thorough check, he needed to keep his focus on his work.

Finally finished repairing the damaged wheel, Lyle closed the large doors to his blacksmith's shop. He needed to do a thorough check, and did not wish for looky-loos. There were far too many gossips in this town, and they weren't all old ladies who passed on every skerrick of information they came across. It was more than frustrating – it was downright annoying.

Lyle removed his gloves and leather apron, then began his search. He opened every cupboard, looked under every table, and even checked inside an old trunk he kept for storing offcuts. There was nothing out of place.

Still not convinced he had imagined it, Lyle continued to search. There was only one place left to search, and that was his home. Meagre as it was, it was his pride and joy, and it was where he spent his time when he wasn't working.

The small cottage was located on the same property as his blacksmith's shop and was built by Lyle's father. It was not a large building and had only two bedrooms, but it was all Lyle needed.

Bracing himself for what he might find, Lyle found his reluctance to open the door quite strange. He'd never been afraid before. But then again, he'd never been faced with a situation such as this one before.

He reached for the door handle, only to discover the door was open ever so slightly. His heart pounded, which shocked him. Lyle was normally calm, no matter the situation. Even that time he'd been badly burned as a young boy learning the trade, he had not panicked. His father calmly explained what to do, enabling him to keep a cool head.

Except this was different. It was a case of someone invading his private abode. At least that's what Lyle believed. He reached for his Colt, his hand shaking. Not once in his life had Lyle needed to use his firearm.

Oh, he knew how to use it – his father had seen to that. He'd also ensured his young son understood that once you shot and killed a man, there was no going back. "Who's there?" he said quietly. Lyle knew he sounded weak, and that would never do. "Show yourself," he said, this time more confidently, his voice firm.

His head spun around as he heard the slightest movement. He stepped in the direction of the sound. It seemed to come from the kitchen. Or more precisely, the pantry. He moved swiftly, but quietly.

Minute sound pricked his ears. The intruder was definitely in there.

It was too loud to be a rodent, but too soft to be a human. What he was dealing with, Lyle did not know. He held the Colt tightly in his shaking hands. Stepping into the pantry, shock punched the breath from his lungs. This was not what he expected to find.

"Who are you?" he asked, keeping his voice low. "And what are you doing in my home?" The urge to holster his gun was strong, but until he knew the woman's intent, he would do no such thing.

She stared at him but didn't speak. Tears swam in her eyes, but they didn't fall. She'd rolled herself into a ball, as though trying to hide herself away. Except it wasn't possible. She should have chosen better. Lyle mentally shook himself. What a foolish thing to think!

"I…" Her voice wavered and was barely audible. She closed her eyes tightly as though forcing all bad thoughts away. When she opened them again, those unshed tears rolled down her face.

His heart thudded. Had he caused her tears? Had the vision of him wielding a gun caused her distress? He wanted nothing more but to rid himself of the Colt and crouched low. Except it could be a trap and he would be the one in real trouble.

He stared into her eyes. Her big blue eyes flooded with tears. Lyle watched as she licked her dry lips.

Now she unfurled herself and sat upright. She straightened her shoulders and stared directly into his face. "I apologize," she said, her voice firm but wavering. "I didn't mean to involve you. I simply had to hide. To get away."

It was then she stood. Lyle stood with her. This tiny woman, who didn't even reach his shoulders, had found not only her voice, but her gumption.

She tried to push past him, but he stiffened and blocked her retreat. "Who are you, and what are you doing here?" he asked firmly.

The woman flinched. "I'm hiding from murderers," she said, her voice barely above a whisper.

Any thought of holstering his gun left Lyle's mind. This woman was in danger, and it was his job to help her.

How he would do that was another thing altogether.

"Let me see if I've got this right," Lyle said as he sat opposite the intruder. "Two men, who you don't know and have no idea what they look like, murdered your father. Then they came to your house and tried to kill you." He studied her, this woman who said her name was Peggy Martin.

She seemed genuine, and he had no reason not to believe her. Unless she was an actress and putting on a show, Peggy was petrified of what would happen if those men found her. Pulling out the journal from the front of her gown seemed to strengthen her words. He hadn't seen inside the journal, nor did he want to.

The best thing he could do now was get the sheriff involved. Except Peggy didn't want to do that. He was facing a losing battle – she was a grown woman who had a mind of her own.

"Father was elderly," she said quietly. "He'd recently retired to live the rest of his life in peace. He was gunned down in the middle of town." Tears filled her eyes again. Her father's death was still raw, because he'd died only days ago.

"You didn't know about any illegal activities he'd undertaken?" He didn't want to ask, but Lyle knew he had to do so. Determining Peggy's innocence was important to him.

She stared at him in anger. "I had no idea. If I knew, I would have put a stop to it." She pursed her lips and Lyle understood how angry she really was. His mother did the same thing when she was not happy about something either Lyle or his father said.

He held up his hands in defense. "The safest thing would be to take the journal to the sheriff." Lyle watched her reaction. She seemed confused. Her confusion made him rethink the situation. Did she believe the law was involved in this…murderous spree? He studied her closely. It was clear Peggy was afraid. It was also evident she didn't know what to do.

They could visit the sheriff's office – Lyle did not believe the sheriff here in town was tainted. Not that he'd had a lot of interaction with the man. He ran a clean town, and any criminal activity was given short shrift.

"My father was a good man," Peggy said forcefully. "He would never do such a thing under his own volition." She closed her eyes, and Lyle could see she was trying to calm herself. "Not once in my thirty-six years have I known my father to do anything untoward. Except his journal says otherwise." Her voice broke on the last sentence. "He was coerced, according to what he wrote."

"At least you have evidence he was coerced. That's got to mean something."

"Have you always lived with your father?" Lyle had to ask. If Peggy was away for long periods of time, she may not know the truth about her father's activities. "The only time I left home was when I left to train as a nurse. I returned to work at the local hospital. The same hospital where Father worked."

"You didn't hear any rumors about…"

"No!" she said firmly, interrupting his questioning. "My father was a good man. Until he wasn't." Her voice became a whisper. The situation seeming to weigh on her shoulders.

"Something like that would be kept quiet. Few people would know about it." He was only guessing now, but Lyle was certain it would be the case. To be successful at something like this, the less people who knew, the better.

He wasn't certain whether the killers were aware of the journal's existence. With every occurrence recorded by Peggy's father. Not only names and dates, but details of exactly how he had ended the lives of those men when ordered to do so.

Chapter Three

Peggy was rendered speechless.

Even after briefly reading the journal, she wasn't convinced her father had done this. Except it was his writing in the journal.

And now he was dead and buried. If he hadn't been involved, he would still be alive. Wouldn't he?

Why those men came after her, Peggy did not know. Unless… She sighed. Unless they discovered the existence of her father's journal. Or guessed it existed. That in itself would be enough to ensure they got their hands on the evidence and eliminate her in the process.

She was a loose end. It was no wonder they wanted to kill her.

Peggy shook her head. No matter what she did now, she was a sitting duck. She couldn't go out on the street, but she equally didn't want to put this man, Lyle Peterson, in danger. He was trying to help her, but in the process, she'd implicated him.

A small cry left her lips.

"What is it?" he asked urgently.

She shook her head. "I shouldn't have come here. Going straight to the sheriff's office would have been smarter. Now you are at risk."

He reached out and covered her hand. "Don't worry yourself about me. I can handle myself." Peggy wasn't sure if Lyle was offended by her words, but he certainly wasn't happy with her declaration.

The truth was, she *had* put him in danger. Of all the places she could have chosen to hide, she had to come here. Lyle was nothing but kind and caring. She'd only ended up here because the stagecoach driver had believed this town, Granville, was a good place to hide.

He'd taken them around the back of the stagecoach depot to water and feed the horses and told her how to get into town without being seen. To her surprise it worked.

The first building she spotted was the blacksmiths. It was reasonably large, and she thought it a good place to hide. The blacksmith was busy doing whatever blacksmiths do and wouldn't see her enter. The shield he wore on his face saw to that.

"I should go," she said, her voice wavering. "No matter what you say, I know my being here has put you at risk. These men would not even blink at killing you to get what they want. They've done it many times before."

Instead of replying, Lyle glanced at the clock on the wall. "It's lunch time. You must be hungry. I know I am." He stood then and headed toward the kitchen, leaving Peggy dumbfounded. One minute they are talking about murderers, and the next he's worrying about his stomach.

She blinked. Was he really so distanced from what was going on in his own home? Peggy made a snap decision to leave. The only problem was she had to get past him in the kitchen. As far as she could tell, it was the only way in and out of the cottage.

Her mind made up, Peggy stood and made her way to the kitchen. She moved slowly and silently – it was the only way she would get past Lyle without his knowledge. The issue would be the front door. How did she open it without him hearing her leave?

Peggy halted, then removed her boots and held them tightly. She would put them back on once she was outside. When she reached the kitchen, Lyle was working at the kitchen counter. What he was doing, she wasn't certain. But she would get past him without Lyle's knowledge. That much was clear.

Halfway through the kitchen, she was grabbed. Peggy screamed except no sound came out of her mouth. Lyle leaned into her. "I'll take my hand away if you promise not to scream. You don't want the entire town to know you're here, do you?"

Her heart pounded, and she shook her head. It was the last thing she wanted. Or needed. Peggy was trying to hide, after all.

He slowly removed his hand and released his grip on her. Peggy's immediate thought went to trying to escape his clutches. Her heart continuing to pound, her mind was jumbled. Lyle was not her enemy; he was trying to protect her.

"I thought we had an agreement," he said, a frown marring his face. "You were to stay hidden here." She opened her mouth to speak, but he interrupted her. "Don't you dare say you are worried about me. I am more concerned about you."

He stared down into her face, his fear for her clear. Now he'd made her feel guilty. Peggy wasn't sure what to do.

"Promise me you won't run again. Those men could be here in town for all you know."

Peggy knew he was right, and it made her heart pound harder. So much she felt lightheaded. She snatched at the front of his shirt before she could fall to the floor.

~*~

This wasn't right. Peggy wasn't in the wrong. She had always followed the rule of the land and was a law-abiding citizen. Until today, she believed her father was, too.

Except now she knew differently.

Her hand went to her chest. Peggy needed to assure herself the journal was still safely tucked away inside her shirt. Panic hit when she couldn't feel its presence. Where was it? When had she lost it?

As she opened her eyes, Peggy found herself in a strange place. Laying on a bed she was unfamiliar with. "It's alright," Lyle said gently, and she felt relieved. His kind voice helped Peggy to remember what went on before this moment. She was no longer concerned for her safety. Not at this moment anyway.

"Where is the…" She stopped mid-sentence. Peggy sensed someone else in the room.

"Ma'am," the stranger said. "I am Doc Huggins. You appear to be suffering from exhaustion. You need to rest, and you'll be right as rain." Peggy stared at the stranger. He wasn't wrong – she was exhausted, but there was far more he didn't know. "Now, Lyle," the doctor continued. "Let me see that burn. It is, after all, the reason I came here."

"It certainly was good timing," Lyle said. His voice was soothing, and it calmed Peggy at the very moments she needed reassurance.

Peggy watched as the doctor removed a bandage from Lyle's wrist, then studied it. He added salve to the burn, then rewrapped it. "Another couple of days and you'll never know it was there."

Lyle chuckled. "I doubt that, Doc. The proof is in all these other scars."

"Prevention is better than cure," the doc said as he finished his house call and prepared to leave.

Lyle shrugged. Peggy hadn't noticed the scars before, but now she did. They weren't huge, but there were several scars on each arm, all around the same area. "I'll see what I can do, Doc."

Doc Huggins sighed. "It's all I ask. Look after your cousin, and make sure she rests."

Cousin? In her confused state of mind, it was on Peggy's lips to question the doctor's assumption of who she was. Perhaps, though, Lyle had told him a little white lie to cover up her existence.

She was beginning to understand Lyle was someone she could trust.

Chapter Four

Lyle was relieved to see Doc Huggins leave. The timing was near perfect. He'd only moments earlier laid Peggy on his bed after she'd fainted.

Despite the main door to his workshop being closed, he hadn't locked it, and the doc let himself in. As he always did.

With the disruption of earlier, with this interloper in his workshop, he'd forgotten the doc was coming today. It was an arrangement they'd made some time ago. Every time he burned himself, which was regularly, Lyle would take himself off to the doctor's office. For subsequent visits, the doc came to him.

Like the doc kept telling him, he needed to stop getting burned. He had burns on burns, that had also been burned in the past. His skin was gnarly – not that the sight of it bothered him, but it hurt like the dickens.

"You told him I was your cousin?" Peggy's voice startled him. "I guess that was better than the truth."

Lyle turned to face his guest. "I couldn't think of another feasible explanation on the spur of the moment."

He watched as she scanned his arms. "That's a lot of burns you have there," she said quietly. "Doc was right – prevention is far better than…"

"Not you, too," he interrupted, but regretted his outburst. The hurt expression on her face was more than he could bear. "I apologize," Lyle said. "The doc tells me the same thing every time I get a burn like this one."

"How many don't you treat?" she asked quietly.

It was as though she could read his mind. There were plenty he didn't have treated. Why bother when they were so small?

"Let me see," she said as she slowly sat up, and balanced herself on the edge of the bed. Her soft hands reached out and held his before he had a chance to protest. She pushed his long sleeves further up his arms and studied each scar, then ran a finger across each one. "This is ridiculous," she said firmly. "You are a grown man and need to look after yourself better than this."

If the situation wasn't so serious, it would be laughable. Not the scars – that wasn't what he meant. It was Peggy checking out his scars, then telling him off for having them. Something niggled at the back of his mind.

What would she know about scars? "You're a…doctor?" he asked cautiously. She shook her head. "You're a nurse." This time it wasn't a question. He was certain of the answer.

She frowned. "Didn't we discuss this earlier? I told you I was a trained nurse and worked at the hospital."

She did, that much was true, but there was no mention she was a nurse. Was there? What Lyle thought she did there, he wasn't certain. What he did know was his brain was quite befuddled. He hated to think what was going through Peggy's mind right now. "Did we?" he asked, still uncertain. "Anyway, burns are a hazard of the trade. My father had the same set of scars."

He heard her sigh. Frustration? Probably, but there was nothing he could do about it. "If you are feeling better, I need to get back to work soon. I don't normally close for this long."

She scowled. "You haven't eaten. It's not good to go without food."

Lyle scratched his head. Now she was giving him health advice? "I have a customer coming for his wheel in…" He glanced up at the clock. "An hour," he finished.

Peggy stood up. He glanced down into her face. She was quite pretty when she didn't frown or scowl. "Then you have almost an hour," she said, and pushed him toward the kitchen.

This tiny woman was manhandling him. He couldn't help but chuckle.

"What's so funny?" she demanded. It was clear she was used to bossing people around. Sick people no less.

"Nothing, I'm certain," he said, trying to keep his voice free of all emotion, then headed to the kitchen.

~*~

Although hurried, lunch was enjoyable. Lyle was used to eating alone, and hadn't thought having company would make a difference. And yet it did. Peggy finished preparing the meal he'd begun making earlier, and he made their beverages. Coffee for him, and tea for Peggy.

She seemed a gentle person on the surface, but it was already clear to Lyle she could also be fierce when necessary. It made him want to wind back the clock and get know Peggy before her life was in danger.

Then her father would still be alive. It made him wonder what sort of man William Martin was. What kind of father he was. According to Peggy, he was a kind man, and she had no reason to question his motives.

Until he was gunned down on the street, she suspected nothing untoward.

Peggy Martin was a brave woman. That much was true. Staying behind to find whatever it was her father had hidden, and not even knowing what that was? She could have been killed.

Lyle didn't look in the journal. It was far better he didn't know what it contained. His next task was to decide how to handle the situation. Should he get the sheriff involved, or find another way to ensure Peggy's safety?

Her biggest concern was dirty lawmen. Granville's sheriff had only been here two years at most. It didn't make him untrustworthy, but it meant Lyle had no idea if the man could be trusted or should be avoided at all costs.

He watched as Peggy moved about his kitchen. It had been a long time since a woman had graced this cottage. His mother was the last female to live here. Once she had died, his home became a cold and emotionless place.

Father tried his best, but nothing could replace the happiness his mother brought to their home. Despite the difficult circumstances, having Peggy here seemed to change all that. At this late stage of his life, Lyle had not thought of marriage – after all, what woman would want a man on the wrong side of forty?

It was not something he'd even thought about for many years.

He shook himself mentally. Peggy was only here until other arrangements could be made. If he had his way, Lyle would ensure the sheriff took control of the situation later today. The last thing he needed was a distraction from his work.

The woman currently in his kitchen was the biggest distraction he could ever remember having – in his entire life.

Chapter Five

Peggy realized her life was still in danger, but felt somewhat more relaxed in Lyle's company. His kitchen was cozy and easy to get around. The soup he'd begun heating on the stove looked good, and the aroma was enticing.

She wondered if he'd made the bread himself, but dismissed the thought almost immediately. Anyone could make soup, but bread was a different thing altogether. Besides, when would he have time?

It appeared he ran a demanding business, so time would be of the essence. She concluded bread making would be the last thing on his mind. Turning to face him, Peggy's eyes drifted to the bandage on his wrist.

Why did men dismiss the most important thing there was – their health? More women attended the hospital than men, until it was too late. Women went willingly, men were often dragged in unrelenting.

Peggy shook herself mentally. Why she was worrying about the blacksmith, she had no idea. If he involved the sheriff as he'd suggested, she would be gone by the end of the day. For some unknown reason, it pulled at her heart. She felt comfortable here, and Peggy had no idea why.

Perhaps it was because the cottage sat behind the locked doors of the blacksmith's workshop, preventing unwanted visitors from entering the premises. Or maybe it was due to the man himself. Peggy's mind was in confusion. She was still trying to process the fact someone wanted her dead.

In hindsight, it would have been better to leave the journal behind. They would have found it, then left Peggy alone. At least that would be the hope. Except these were paid killers. Hired guns.

Trying to murder her. Peggy Martin.

And for what reason? Her father got himself mixed up in the wrong crowd? Peggy had only read a small portion of her father's journal, but she'd seen enough to know he was coerced into killing certain patients at the hospital. For what reason, she may never know.

She couldn't imagine what would entice him to murder, not once, but many times over a number of years.

"Come and sit down." Lyle's soothing voice pulled her out of her dark thoughts. "You need to eat something."

She tried to muster up a smile, but wasn't sure she quite managed to pull it off. "I'm not hungry," she said quietly. She truly wasn't. All this murderous escapade going on around her had drained her appetite.

Lyle stood and took the few steps toward her. "You are incredibly pale," he said. "Not to mention skinny."

Her head shot up. "I'm not skinny!" she barked. "I'm just small boned." Her heart was pounding at her indignant rebuff. How rude of him to presume her to be ill. After all, that was the implication, wasn't it?

"How long is it since you ate anything?" he demanded to know.

Peggy had to think about it. She'd only snacked on bread and cheese after her father's untimely death but hadn't eaten anything substantial since. There was no longer anyone around to notice, so it had passed by without interference.

In other words, she was alone in the world. It was the first time in her entire life she was completely alone. Realization hit hard. It meant she was now an orphan. She might be a woman past her prime, but it didn't alter the fact she'd lost both her parents.

She was numb, and couldn't think straight. Lyle's hands were on her shoulders. He guided her to the table, where he sat her down. "You must eat," he said firmly. "Otherwise you'll faint again, and I'll have to get the doc back."

It was the last thing she wanted. Knowing what doctors were like, he would immediately assume she was with child, and that was the farthest thing from the truth.

She reached out and took a mouthful of tea. It was good. The aroma of the soup right in front of her was enticing, and she leaned in to get a better whiff of it.

"Eat up," Lyle said gently. "It's good food. Mary Simpson at the mercantile made it. She's an excellent cook."

Lyle didn't make the soup? For some strange reason, it made her chuckle. Then she began laughing, and Peggy couldn't stop. She knew what this was – hysteria. After everything she'd endured over the past few days, it was no wonder. She'd kept everything bottled up inside of her, even at her father's funeral.

Tears now flooded her face, even while she continued to laugh. Where this would all lead, Peggy had no idea. What she did know was it needed to be over soon, or she would lose her sanity.

Without looking, she knew Lyle's eyes were on her. A shiver went down her spine, and she glanced at him. At first, he appeared shocked, then he stood and came to her. Squatting down next to her, he put an arm around her, and held Peggy tight.

She didn't push him away, and didn't complain. Hysteria was a real thing, and it could quickly get out of control. Her hysterical laughter had turned to sobbing, and he pulled her close. Lyle didn't tell her to stop, nor did he make any disparaging remarks. He simply let her get it all out of her system.

Peggy knew it was what she needed. It was the first time she had truly cried for her father. For the way he'd died, and even the fact his life was taken far too soon.

Now she had to worry about her own safety, and while ever she stayed here at the blacksmith's cottage, Lyle's safety as well.

He pulled out a handkerchief and handed it to her. When Peggy didn't take it, Lyle wiped at her tears. He pushed her unruly hair behind her ears, and held her close.

This complete stranger cared more for her than most other people she'd know for the majority of her life. How could that be? Why would a stranger have more compassion for her than those from her home town?

Few of her father's colleagues and friends attended his funeral. It was mostly a handful of her nursing friends. Did that mean the others knew of his illegal behavior and turned a blind eye? That he'd been murdering patients when told to do so?

Peggy shook herself mentally. She couldn't get her head around her father doing such a thing. There must have been extenuating circumstances for him to even consider cooperating with such orders.

Otherwise, Peggy didn't know her father. Didn't know him at all.

Lyle loosened his grip on her, but was still right by her side. Peggy stared into his face, drawn to his brown eyes. They were soulful, and she felt calm whenever he was near. Why, she didn't know.

Lyle suddenly stood, stretching himself out. Without a word, he pulled his chair from the other side of the table to be next to hers. He slid his food across, and urged her to eat. When she didn't move, he lifted her spoon and began to feed her.

Peggy was stunned. Why did he even care? They were thrown together, and the minute he involved the sheriff, she would never see him again.

The mere thought of it shattered her heart.

Chapter Six

Lyle knew moving close to Peggy was the right thing to do. Even if his heart was pounding from her closeness. At least that's what he assumed was causing it to beat so loudly like this. He could barely hear himself think.

Still, if it helped her feel safer and cared for, that's all that mattered. No doubt the sheriff would want to take her into his care the moment he heard her story.

He lifted the spoon to her mouth, and Peggy stared at him in shock. It wasn't often he hand fed his visitors, but the circumstances of the day warranted it. At least that's what Lyle told himself. Otherwise, it was blatantly clear she had no intention of eating. Peggy had been unable to tell him when she last ate a decent meal. Not that soup and bread could be considered decent, but it was better than nothing.

If he hadn't already bought those items, Lyle knew he'd be dishing up beans to his guest. And that would never do. It was not a meal the ladies seemed to like. He couldn't begin to wonder why.

Without warning, her hand closed around his. Her skin was soft, and her touch gentle. It sent a shiver down his spine. He glanced into her face. Peggy's expression had changed – it had now softened. She appeared to have settled, which is what he wanted. Her distress was almost unbearable.

She opened her mouth to speak, but instead licked her lips. "I'm sorry," she said quietly. "This is the first time I have truly grieved for the loss of my father. The anger I felt for the way he died simply took over." Tears pooled in her eyes, and Lyle wondered how much more anguish she could take.

She swiped at her cheeks as tears fell again. Only this time they were short-lived. The worst was over, he was certain.

He placed the spoon back in her bowl. "No need to apologize," he said gently. "Grieving is important. I'm glad I was here to support you in your time of need," he said, then admonished himself. It sounded as though he believed the role he played was important, when in reality, it wasn't. He was simply in the right place at the right time when he was needed.

"You need to eat," Peggy said, mimicking his words. "And you need to do it soon. It won't be long before your customer will arrive?"

A small smile crossed his face. Peggy was right – his customer was due soon, but was it safe to leave her alone, or would she dissolve into a uncontrollable mess like before? He was torn between loyalty to his customer, and his obligation to his guest.

"Don't worry about me. I promise I won't go anywhere. I'll wash the dishes and clean up in here while you're gone." She smiled then, despite her puffy eyes and red nose. "That has to be a bonus, right?"

"Of course. It's not often a beautiful woman offers to clean house for me." He couldn't help but grin, and it made him feel so much better. "I'll eat if you do," he said, and was pleasantly surprised when she did.

His words elicited a smile, which sent warmth soaring through him. He couldn't put into words the joy he felt when Peggy picked up her spoon and began to eat the thick and tasty vegetable soup.

He pushed the butter dish toward her, as well as the bread he'd already sliced. Peggy glanced at him, and he was certain she was waiting for him to begin eating as well.

"The soup is good," she said quietly, between mouthfuls. She frowned momentarily before speaking again. "Now that I think about it, apart from some bread and cheese, I don't believe I've eaten anything much at all. Since father died, that is."

It took all his effort not to gasp. "When was that? Two days ago?" he asked quietly, trying not to show his concern.

Peggy shook her head, then frowned. "It was three days ago. At least I think it was. I've lost track of time."

No wonder she didn't know what day it was. So much had happened in those few days – all of them life changing. Lyle couldn't help but wonder what the next few days, and even weeks, held in store for her.

They finished eating, and after checking the time, Lyle knew he had to leave her alone. "My customer will be here shortly," he said. "I really must go and open the door." He began to walk away, but turned back to face her. "You will be fine here by yourself, won't you?" he asked, then reached for her hand.

The strangest feeling came over him. It wasn't anything Lyle had experienced before. He didn't want to leave her alone. Didn't want to meet with the customer despite the man waiting for his wagon wheel to be repaired so he and his family could continue their journey.

Covering her hand with his own, Lyle felt his heart tug. It was nothing like he'd ever experienced before.

"I will be fine, I promise," Peggy told him firmly. "Off you go and do your blacksmith thing."

His blacksmith thing? Her words almost had him laughing. It was easy to tell she was a nurse. She was used to bossing patients around, and was trying it on him.

Except it wouldn't work. If he didn't have a customer waiting for him, Lyle would have stayed right there in his kitchen. Wouldn't he?

"Go on, then," she urged, then gathered up the soiled dishes and took them to the sink. He hated to leave her like this, but work called.

Lyle left the kitchen feeling as though he was letting her down. Except Peggy had made it very clear he was not required.

In his own kitchen! Had he just been dismissed from his very own cottage by a woman he'd known for a matter of hours? It gave him the strangest feeling. He was convinced he could trust her, despite everything.

The moment he handed over the wheel, he would lock up for the day. He had no pressing jobs, and he needed to contact the sheriff. The rest of his day depended on what the sheriff had to say.

As he unlocked the door to his workshop, Lyle noticed two men on the other side of the road. They were complete strangers to him, and the hair on the back of his neck stood up. He was not prepared to leave Peggy alone to visit the sheriff while those strangers loitered nearby. Or even while they were in town.

They looked as though they'd slept in the same clothes for days. In addition, Lyle had feelings of untrustworthiness about them. What he would do now, he wasn't sure. But he did know, he would not leave Peggy alone or pass her off to anyone else.

She was his responsibility now.

Chapter Seven

Peggy set about cleaning up Lyle's kitchen. It wasn't a task she loved, but she couldn't stand a messy kitchen.

It didn't take long, and she felt a sense of satisfaction once she finished. Then she decided to explore his pantry. Perhaps if she could make herself useful, he might let her stay. The man was clearly incapable of cooking even the simplest meal, so doing it for him might show Lyle she was worth holding on to for a while.

Even a day or two would work. Long enough to ensure those men were not in town. The stagecoach driver, Caleb was his name, was very kind. If it hadn't been for him, she wouldn't be here now. He'd told her how to get to the main street without being seen, and advised her to find a place that looked large enough to hide in. He suggested either the livery or the blacksmith's shop.

Failing that, he said, look for a man who appeared strong and determined. Someone who would help her no matter what. Her only other options, Caleb believed, were to stay on the stagecoach longer, or get herself to one of the outlying ranches. It would be harder to find her there, he suggested.

Except how did she get to a ranch? She dismissed that almost immediately. Not that her mind was working as it should be, but being here in Lyle's home? She felt calm. More relaxed than she'd been for days.

Peggy stood at the doorway of Lyle's pantry. It was far from full. She found a large bag of flour, a small amount of sugar, and a dozen eggs. In the icebox was a bottle of milk, cream and bacon. There was enough here to make pancakes for supper. It was then she spotted a few potatoes and onions.

Perfect.

She relocated all the ingredients to the kitchen, then looked for the bowls and other utensils she would need. It was far too early to begin making the pancakes now, but she could make a dessert of some kind.

Peggy tried to recall what other ingredients were in the pantry. She closed her eyes and tried to visualize the small room. With her nerves at their peak, she couldn't think, so instead returned to the pantry.

She didn't think Lyle would mind if she took his last two apples. Especially since he would have a sweet dessert for supper. As of now, the pantry was almost bare, so he would need to buy supplies from the mercantile tomorrow. That was, if he wanted her to continue to stay here. Peggy knew she wasn't the greatest cook in the world, but her cooking was passable.

Father had not complained, not even once, since Mother had passed. The alternative was to eat at the diner every night, but it would have been far too expensive.

She opened the bag of flour gingerly, hoping weevils had not taken over. Peggy held her breath the entire time, and was relieved to find no sign of the horrid creatures.

Ensuring there was enough flour for both the pancakes and an apple cake, Peggy began measuring the ingredients for the dessert. Flour and sugar first, double-checking there was still enough for the main course.

She was confused though – if Lyle didn't cook for himself, why have any ingredients in the pantry? Perhaps he had a lady friend who visited and made meals for him from time to time. Peggy really didn't know, and was only assuming.

With all the ingredients ready all she needed now was a cake tin. Her heart thudded. What if there wasn't one? She rifled through the cupboards. "Thank goodness," she said out loud. The words meant only for her own ears.

"Thank goodness for what?" Lyle's voice startled her, and Peggy almost spilled the ingredients out of the bowl she'd mixed them in.

Hand to her heart, she breathed a sigh of relief. Before she had a chance to answer, Lyle's eyes went to the untidy mess she had on the counter top. "What's going on here?" he asked, his voice full of curiosity.

"I'm preparing supper," she said, her voice wavering. Would he be angry with her for using the last of his ingredients? Peggy hoped not.

A grin crossed his face. "I don't know what it is, but it looks good." He took a few steps forward and glanced into the cake tin, his grin even wider now.

"It's apple cake," Peggy said. "I…I used the last of your apples. I hope you don't mind." She glanced down, not wanting to look at him. Would Lyle be annoyed she'd used up his sparse pantry items?

"Don't you dare apologize," he said firmly. "I will never refuse good food." His eyes went to the remaining ingredients behind her. "What is that about?" he asked, his hand motioning toward the counter top.

"Pancakes with fried potatoes and onions? Is that alright?" she asked, not sure how he would react.

"Alright? It is the best news I've heard in a very long time. Most of my meals come from the mercantile or the diner. Otherwise out of a can." She glanced up to see his grin was even wider. "Baked beans that is. I am rather sick of them," he added.

Peggy smiled, then added the cake to the oven. It needed to go on soon, otherwise it wouldn't be ready in time. "Did your customer turn up on time?" Peggy asked as she closed the oven door.

"He did," Lyle told her. He sat down at the table, and Peggy made coffee for him. "I'm not used to this," he said. "Living alone, I have to do everything for myself."

She wanted to say not anymore, but Peggy could not assume anything. As far as she was aware, Lyle could have already alerted the sheriff.

It meant she may not even be here when her cake was ready, or to make Lyle's supper. Peggy didn't want to think about it. She was enjoying the time spent with him, and didn't want it to end.

He took a mouthful of coffee, then glanced up at her. "I have to tell you something," he said gently.

Peggy knew what was coming. The sheriff was coming to take her away. Her heart shattered. She was feeling at home here. Comfortable with the blacksmith, even if he didn't want her here. "The sheriff is coming," she said quietly, her chin in the air. If it was the last thing she did, Peggy would not show any emotion. Wouldn't let him know it would hurt to go.

"It's not that," Lyle said, his face covered in confusion. "I saw two men. Complete strangers across the street."

Peggy gasped. Were they the two killers who'd come to her home?

"I'm not risking telling the sheriff yet. You can stay here tonight, and we'll decide what to do tomorrow. Does that sound feasible to you? Please tell me if you would prefer to leave immediately."

Her heart pounded far harder than it had before. The men who murdered her father had found her. How could they have done so? The stagecoach driver seemed genuinely concerned for her welfare. Surely, he wasn't one of them? The implications had her reeling.

She staggered across the room and sat down opposite Lyle. "I don't want to leave," she whispered.

Lyle reached across the table and covered her hand. "In that case, you will stay here as long as it takes."

Peggy had never been so relieved in her life.

Chapter Eight

Lyle didn't want to leave Peggy alone. Not while she was in a state of panic, as she was now. He should have known better than to mention the strangers on the street. They were across the road, opposite his shop. It seemed clear to Lyle they were looking for Peggy.

Still, he could be wrong.

The best thing he could do now was close up shop for the remainder of the day, and ensure her safety. What she'd been through was horrific. He had an awful feeling it would get worse before it got better.

Why her father hadn't gone to the law about his circumstances, Lyle didn't know. Unless… He shook himself mentally. There was only one reason he could think of, and that was a dirty sheriff.

Was Plainville run by criminals? It was something to keep in mind. Otherwise, how was Peggy's father manipulated for so long? The size of the journal indicated his participation had been going on for a very long time.

There was only one thing Lyle could think of that would force an upstanding doctor to cooperate with lowdown skunks.

They threatened his daughter.

Lyle was no lawman, never had been, never would be, but it made perfect sense to him. If a man wouldn't do what was asked of him, find the thing he valued most. In this case, Peggy. It made him wonder if she had worked it out.

Most likely not. Surely she would have mentioned it if she had. He shook himself mentally. Now he wondered if the sheriff here in Granville was dirty, too. Could the man be trusted? Lyle truly did not know, and wasn't willing to put Peggy's life on the line to find out. Instead, he would make other inquiries. But he would need to be discreet, otherwise those looking for Peggy would find her. And that would never do.

An idea began to form in his mind, but Lyle knew it would be tricky to pull off. It would also mean he had to leave Peggy alone while he carried it out. He would have to think more on the dilemma of the journal. It needed to be concealed. It was likely what the killers were after, and he was certain if they found it with Peggy, they would not hesitate to murder her. Tying up loose ends was presumably why her father had died.

His mind was in overload, and Lyle knew he had to stop thinking. Instead, he watched Peggy as she prepared the evening meal. One thing he knew for certain – he was enjoying Peggy's company, and it had nothing to do with food.

~*~

The aroma filling the small cottage when the oven door was finally opened filled Lyle with heartwarming memories. His mother was a fine cook, and going by the smell in the kitchen right now, Peggy was too.

He hadn't left her side from the moment he returned after locking up the store. It wasn't unusual for him to close the store when he had no one waiting for orders. He worked for himself and set his own hours. It was true he worked far too much. He'd been told far too many times by his customers.

Lately he'd been feeling his age, and was taking more time off than previously. He knew it was more a case of long hours and hard work, than age related. Protecting Peggy was the excuse he needed to slow down. He didn't see her situation as a good one, but it forced him to do the right thing by them both. "It smells delicious," he said, breathing in the enticing aroma. "It's a long time since desserts or cakes were made in this kitchen."

Sympathy crossed Peggy's face. "Your mother?" she asked her voice wavering. "I lost my mother, too. It's not easy," she said.

Lyle felt her pain, and wanted to ease it. Except he didn't know how. "Why don't we move into the sitting room?" he asked, avoiding the question. Besides, it was far more comfortable there. The moment he entered, it was clear he needed to refuel the fire. The winter had set in and the cottage became quite chilly, not only at night, but also during the day.

Peggy had no luggage, and only had the clothes on her back, a thick coat, and her reticule. He recalled his father's refusal to give away mother's possessions, and wondered if any of her belongings would work for Peggy.

After his father had passed, Lyle moved both their clothes and other belongings to what was now the spare room. Formerly, it was Lyle's room. As he added more logs to the fire, these thoughts filled his mind. This was the reason he needed to work less hours – thoughts were constantly racing through his mind. Doc Huggins had warned him more times than he could remember – if he didn't slow down, both his body and mind would pull him into old age far too quickly.

It was almost laughable. Lyle was already old. Forty had passed a couple of years earlier. Already Lyle considered himself old, but in the scheme of things, he wasn't really that old. He had to admit there were days when he felt like an old man. Blacksmithing was not easy on the body. Not when you pushed yourself to the limit, as he did on a daily basis.

Satisfied with the now fiercely burning fire, Lyle stood. Stretching himself out, he felt the pangs of his work. Taking it easy, as the doc suggested, was probably a good idea. He didn't have to work long hours to keep his business afloat, so why was he being so stubborn?

"Let me show you the spare room," Lyle said, and guided Peggy there. "It's not huge, but it's comfortable. There are clean sheets on the bed, and the robe is full of my mother's belongings. Help yourself to anything that takes your fancy." He watched her scowl.

Peggy shook her head. "I couldn't do that," she whispered.

But Lyle was determined. "I insist," he said firmly. "Mother has been gone for many years. Her possessions are no longer sentimental." He walked over to the closet and opened both doors. "Father's things are there too. Please. take whatever you want. I really should have donated them to the church. Now I'm glad I didn't." He turned to leave her alone, then turned back to face her. "I will donate father's clothes. It's the right thing to do," he said out loud, making his words a commitment.

He then left the room.

Although thinking about it brought some sadness, Lyle felt a weight had been lifted from his shoulders. Finally making the decision to give away his father's clothes had been cathartic. When Peggy no longer needed or wanted them, he would do the same with Mother's belongings.

It had been pure selfishness on his part in keeping their things. Granville had people in need, just like any other town. Why he hadn't ensured those who needed help were given it, he wasn't sure.

Except Lyle did know. He was holding on to the material things, instead of the memories. For reasons he didn't understand, Peggy's presence here had propelled him into action.

He pondered his future as he sat in the sitting room, taking in the warmth of the fire as he waited for his delightful guest to return.

Chapter Nine

Peggy reluctantly rummaged through the clothes that once belonged to Lyle's mother. They weren't really her style, but beggars can't be choosers as her own mother always said. With no time to pack, and having only a warm coat, her reticule, and the clothes she now wore, Peggy knew she must put aside her reservations and find something suitable.

The clothes were all well-made, and in top condition. They were bright and cheery, and simply looking at them cheered Peggy up somewhat. Her biggest concern was wearing them, and triggering a negative emotion in Lyle.

They were, after all, his mother's clothes.

She sat on the side of the bed, mulling over her options. Lyle had made it blatantly clear from the start he didn't want her here, but now he'd changed his mind. Was it because of the strangers he'd seen on the street?

Peggy had no idea, but she didn't want to stay where she was not wanted. Those men being out there changed things. Without them lurking around, she could have taken the stage out of Granville. Since they were here, no doubt looking for her, Peggy could not venture outside Lyle's cottage.

Apart from the danger it would put her in, if they discovered Lyle had harbored her, he would be a target as well. She couldn't live with herself it that happened. He had been nothing but a gentleman, ensuring her safety. She didn't want to see him killed for helping her. It wouldn't be right.

She was thinking too much. Peggy knew she was. The apple cake would be cool enough to cut, and no doubt Lyle would like to try out her culinary prowess. It wouldn't be long and she would need to start preparing supper.

Pulling herself from the bed, Peggy wished it was as simple pulling herself out of the mental slump she was in. Being pursued by killers was not conducive to a happy life. Her entire life was in turmoil.

How did she get here? She had done nothing wrong. That her father had crossed a line, seemingly some years ago, should not be her legacy. Once a proud doctor who did his utmost to help his patients, when did that change?

She'd read part of the journal, but Peggy was so shell-shocked at what she'd read, she hadn't taken in names or dates. Did she dare do so now?

"Peggy?" Lyle's voice came through the closed door as he lightly tapped. "Are you alright?" He sounded concerned, which confused her. Why did he even care?

"I'm coming," she called, and reluctantly opened the door. Standing on the other side was Lyle. His face marred by a frown. He seemed genuinely concerned for her welfare, which cut to Peggy's heart.

Except she couldn't let herself care for this man. Already she had overstayed her welcome. She'd also put him in grave danger, and that had never been her objective.

Peggy came here to hide. When the coast was clear, she would leave. Lyle was far too astute for her liking, and now it left her with a dilemma.

Did she run and leave him to his life, or stay here until it was truly safe to leave?

"Mmmm, this is so good," Lyle said between mouthfuls. "I'm glad you let me have some before supper."

The apple cake was still warm, and the aroma was enticing, even if Peggy thought so herself. It was a favorite of her father's and she'd made it many times over the years. It was gratifying to know it wasn't only her father singing her praises because she was his daughter.

Lyle did seem to be enjoying the cake, along with the coffee she'd made for him. "You really are an excellent cook," he said when he'd finished.

"Flattery," Peggy said with joy in her heart, "will not get you more cake. She couldn't help but chuckle. Lyle joined her, and warmth filled her. Had she not been in danger, she would not have met Lyle, and wouldn't be sharing such a lighthearted moment with him.

It was strange – both their lives were at risk, and yet both were sharing a small slice of happiness.

Sipping her tea, Peggy pondered her future. If there was such a thing. Safe in her room, the journal lay hidden beneath her mattress. For the time being, at any rate. Was it really the safest place for it? She would speak with Lyle about it, but not now. They were sharing an almost intimate moment, and she didn't want to lose that.

Her heart fluttered whenever he was near, and he filled her with hope. After all these years, she finally met a man she cared about and could even fall in love with. Peggy was in danger, and had pulled him into her ring of danger. It was the last thing she wanted, despite his protests to the contrary.

As though sensing her misgivings, he reached across the table and covered her hand with his. "You will get out of this alive," he whispered, then squeezed her hand.

She gazed into his face. He seemed to genuinely believe his own words. Peggy wasn't so certain. "You don't know that," she said quietly. She knew her words to be true, even if Lyle refused to accept what was staring him in the face.

Lyle stared back at her. "I'm pretty sure I do," he said. "I will protect you, I promise. How many times do I have to say it, before you believe me?" He sounded exasperated, and frankly, Peggy didn't blame him. She felt the same way herself, but for completely different reasons.

She closed her eyes momentarily, attempting to pluck up the courage to say the words. "I should never have come here," she said quietly. "I should have stayed on the stagecoach and gone to goodness knows where."

"Where you would have still needed help," he said firmly, his hand still holding Peggy's. "This is right where you need to be," he said. "I will protect you. We will find a place to hide the journal. Somewhere those men would never think to look."

Peggy frowned. "It's under the mattress."

She was quite frankly annoyed when he broke out into laughter.

62

Chapter Ten

Lyle knew he shouldn't have laughed at Peggy putting the journal under the mattress. She was so naïve, and had no idea it was the first place someone would look. He finally forced himself to stop laughing, but still held her hand. "I apologize," he said. "It was completely rude of me to laugh."

He had to rein in his emotions, or he would laugh again, and that would never do. Peggy was already annoyed. He could see it on her face.

Instead of answering, or even acknowledging his apology, she pulled her hand away. It was the worst punishment she could give, as he now felt hollow. It was as though something he treasured had suddenly disappeared. It was the strangest feeling.

Yes, they had spent a lot of time together, but they didn't know each other. Not really. He knew so little about Peggy, apart from the fact she was running from danger after her father was murdered in broad daylight. He also knew she was a trained nurse.

She knew equally little about him, apart from knowing he was a blacksmith and a bachelor. All that said, Lyle would not object to learning more about Peggy. She seemed kind, scared, and he knew she could cook. She was also stubborn as a mule, and pig-headed. When she wanted to do something, she did it regardless of the consequences.

At least that had been his experience so far.

Just to prove his point, Peggy stood. "I need to prepare for supper," she said. Right in the middle of their conversation, no less. It wasn't that he didn't want pancakes for supper, but he wanted to talk to her about strategies. About where they go from here.

Except Lyle had the impression Peggy didn't want to discuss it further. He understood it could be distressing for her, but if they didn't sort out the details, he would have to take matters into his own hands. "You don't want to discuss it?" he asked, already knowing the answer.

She shook her head, then started to measure out the ingredients. Once she'd mixed the batter, she put it aside and peeled the potatoes and onions.

Peggy didn't speak while she cooked, despite his words, and regardless of him sitting at the table only a few steps away. He sat patiently as she diced the vegetables, then searched the cupboards for a frying pan. At least he assumed that's what she was looking for. "There's a large frying pan under the sink," he told her, "and you'll find a saucepan there too."

She still didn't speak, just waved at him with her back still facing him. It was the strangest behavior Lyle had seen. Not only from Peggy, but from any woman. Not that he had much in the way of dealings with women. Not on a personal basis, anyway.

He was only in the way, at least Lyle decided he was, and pushed his chair back. While pushing his chair in under the table, he studied her. Something wasn't quite right, but he didn't know what it could be.

Then he heard it. Peggy sniffled. Was she crying? He moved to where she stood, and gently placed a hand on her shoulder. "Are you crying?" Lyle asked gently. He never was one for beating around the bush.

She shook her head. "It's the onions," she said quietly. Lyle almost believed her. Then he remembered no matter how badly your eyes watered from onions, it didn't affect you the same way as crying. You didn't sniffle, and your shoulders didn't quiver as hers did now.

Lyle was unsure of his next move. Should he call her out on the lie, or let it be? Except ignoring her distress was not helping anyone. Especially Peggy. "Put down the knife," he said gently, and with a shaking hand, she did as he ordered.

Peggy turned to face him, then glanced up into his face, tears still pouring down her face. "It's all too much," she whispered, and Lyle knew she wasn't referring to the cooking.

She was talking about her father's murder and everything that followed.

Lyle wasn't sure what to do next. His first thought was to wrap her in his arms. He wanted to hold her for as long as it took. But would that be seen as inappropriate? Allowing Peggy to stay in his home already put her in danger of being called out for improper behavior. After all, they were not married.

Not that Lyle had any intention of marrying. He was happily living the life of a bachelor. At least he thought he was. Until he tasted Peggy's cooking. Not to mention when he held her in his arms earlier today.

Did he dare to do so again?

Standing there, glancing down into her face, Lyle felt compelled to hold her. To comfort her. There was something about this woman, apart from her situation, but he couldn't fathom what it was. Yes, she was forthright and opinionated. But she was also beautiful, and something about her had him falling over himself.

Instead of contemplating what to do, he wrapped Peggy in his arms. She rested her head against his chest – he was simply there for her. Lyle lifted a hand and caressed her cheek. She didn't complain and didn't try to stop him. While ever Peggy was comfortable, he would hold her.

This was not what he envisioned for his day. On the other hand, he was certain it would not have been Peggy's idea of the perfect day, either.

Supper was delicious, and it reinforced his belief that Peggy was an excellent cook. Between them, they ate all the pancakes, and not one bit of the vegetables were wasted. They barely spoke during the meal, which suited Lyle fine.

Whenever they discussed her situation, Peggy became distressed. What he could do to help, he wasn't certain. After mulling it over for some time, he decided there was no choice, but to involve the sheriff. Especially since he'd seen the two strangers loitering around nearby.

Darkness was already descending, so if he intended to do anything today, Lyle knew it had to be soon. Apart from worrying about those men breaking in to get to Peggy, if they even knew she was there, he didn't relish leaving her alone. Even with him here with her, Peggy was on edge.

Not that Lyle blamed her. The situation was dire, and she needed constant protection. Except he couldn't do both. Although the sheriff's office wasn't far, and despite being able to lock the main door to the blacksmith's shop, Lyle was loathe to go.

"I am torn," he told Peggy after they'd finished their meal. "I feel the sheriff needs to know what's going on. I also don't want to leave you alone."

Peggy studied him for a few heartbeats, then seemed to make a decision. "If you believe the sheriff can be trusted, you should go. I will be fine here alone."

She didn't sound certain. Her voice wavered, and her face seemed to tense. "Really?" he asked, his heart now pounding. "I'll stay if you'd rather."

Peggy stood and began collecting their soiled dishes. "I'm fine, I promise. I'll keep busy in here. You won't be gone that long, will you?" This time she came across as concerned, although he had to admit she seemed rather calm about it all.

"I am aiming for a short visit with the sheriff. He reached into his holster, and held a gun out to her.

Peggy took a step backwards. "I don't want it," she barked out. "I'd rather take my chances with the frying pan." She smiled briefly, and Lyle felt it was futile to argue. Instead, he headed out.

What or who he would encounter outside of the blacksmith's shop, he didn't know. But Lyle knew he had to have back up of some sort. Otherwise, Peggy would be a sitting duck.

He locked the door the moment he was outside. Dusk had arrived, and glancing around, he couldn't see the two men he'd noticed before. Had they only been passing through town, or were they looking for the woman they wanted to silence?

The question tugged at his heart. What happened to Peggy was unfathomable. Her father had done the wrong thing, that was true. But for Peggy's part, she was innocent. Had she not found her father's ledger, she wouldn't even know what had been going on. She admitted the journal indicated William Martin had murdered several men over a number of years.

He had only recently retired, so was no longer attending patients. Reading between the lines, Lyle believed it was the catalyst to Peggy's father being murdered.

How did you ensure patients did not survive if you no longer practiced medicine? Had he also threatened the killers with exposing them to the law? If that were the case, it made perfect sense. The man must have known it would be the death knell for him, but hadn't planned on his killers going after his daughter.

He might only be a humble blacksmith, but Lyle knew in that moment he would protect Peggy with his own life if necessary.

Lyle didn't know the sheriff well, but he hadn't heard any bad reports about him. Despite that, he felt some apprehension. His head was telling him advising the sheriff was the only way out of this. While his heart told him he needed to be diligent in his interactions with Granville's sheriff.

Chapter Eleven

Peggy stood in the doorway to the cottage and listened for Lyle to lock the main door. Although she expected it, she flinched as she heard the loud click. She did not expect the sound to echo so loudly.

Returning to the kitchen, she wondered why she'd told Lyle she would be fine alone. She wasn't fine. She was shaking – almost as much as when she searched her home for whatever those awful men were looking for. Except back then, she had no idea what it was she needed to find.

Now, though, she had the journal, and had to keep it hidden. She stood at the sink with her hands in the hot water. It felt nice, and helped to calm her. Peggy was petrified right at that moment, but the warm water on her hands had a soothing effect.

It was foolish, this feeling she had. Lyle wasn't far away, and the men he'd seen may not even be the same men chasing her. Peggy hadn't seen their faces, so she wouldn't even be able to recognize them if she came across them.

It was a pitiful situation to be in. If she'd caught even the smallest glimpse, it would be helpful. Not only to her, but also to the sheriff. She resolved to finish washing the dishes and clean the kitchen, and that's exactly what Peggy did. When Lyle returned, he wouldn't be faced with a messy kitchen.

No man deserved that. Peggy's mother had always ensured the house was clean and tidy by the time Father arrived home. Her apron was strategically removed, her hair perfect, and her make up reapplied.

Mother had taught her it was a wife's duty to ensure her husband came home to a clean house, and a happy wife, each and every day. It was not something Peggy wanted to do, but here she was, doing basically the same thing for Lyle. Except he wasn't her husband.

Peggy was startled when she heard the loud click of the door. She hoped it was Lyle returning, and not the killers breaking in. Her heart beat so quickly, she had to sit down. It was then logic took over.

The killers would not have a key.

Only Lyle had a key to his property. But then she heard voices. Had Lyle returned with the sheriff? Peggy hadn't been prepared for him to visit. Not tonight. She supposed it was to be expected. The sheriff would want all the details to set in motion whatever it was he'd need to do.

She placed three mugs on the kitchen counter, her hands shaking. The kettle was almost boiling. The door to the cottage opened, then closed. Peggy jumped yet again. She spun around, almost knocking over the mugs in the process.

Lyle stared at her. "Are you alright?" he said, concern in his voice.

Her hand to her chest, Peggy nodded. "I'll be fine. I was startled, that's all."

Lyle studied her, and she was certain had the sheriff not been there, he might have held her again. She enjoyed being in his arms, and was certain it didn't make him unhappy either.

"Sheriff Virgil Flanagan, meet Peggy Martin."

The sheriff studied her momentarily, then extended his hand. Peggy had little choice but to accept his offer. "Sheriff," she said quietly. "If you both sit down, I'll make coffee. The kettle is on the verge of boiling."

"That's very kind of you, Miss Martin," Sheriff Flanagan said, then sat down at the table.

She placed several slices of cake on a plate, adding them to the center of the table. It wasn't long and the kettle boiled. Peggy diligently made the coffee and gave each man a mug of the hot beverage.

It was then Peggy realized she was doing what her mother always did. Ensuring everything was perfect for the men.

Taking her mug of tea with her, she sat down next to Lyle. He was her only friend in this town, and she didn't think he would mind.

"Miss Martin," the sheriff said.

"Peggy, please." No need to make this harder than it already was.

The sheriff raised his eyebrows, then took a mouthful of coffee. "Lyle has told me about your situation, but I'd like to hear it from you." He studied her then, reminding Peggy of a beady-eyed eagle. His examination of her face made her feel uncomfortable.

As though he understood her misgivings, Lyle reached for her hand under the table. A mere touch from him helped. It gave her comfort, and perhaps even a little confidence to talk to this man who was a complete stranger.

Peggy took a long fortifying breath. "It apparently all started some years ago when my father was approached by criminals," she began. The sheriff listened very carefully to her story, and took copious notes along the way.

After what seemed like hours, Peggy finished her story. Lyle still held her hand, and she didn't complain.

Sheriff Flanagan reached out for a slice of her apple cake, and took a bite. "This is good," he told her. There was no pretense from the sheriff. His official visit was over, and now he would enjoy her hospitality.

It surprised Peggy he hadn't asked to see the journal, but she was glad he didn't. Lyle told her earlier he wasn't certain if the man could be trusted, only because he'd had little to do with him. Peggy decided she had to assume she could rely on him. Otherwise, where would she be without his help?

It was not a good dilemma to be in.

As she continued to sip her tea, Peggy became more relaxed in the sheriff's company. Surely this man could be trusted? The sheriff back home, who was known to be dirty, was a gruff man, and it was easy to see what side of the law he was on.

Sheriff Flanagan was the complete opposite. He was an older man, and appeared to know what he was doing.

"Thank you, Miss… er, Peggy," he said when he'd finished eating. He took a last mouthful of coffee, then stood. "I'll make discreet enquiries, and will get back to you both." He put his hat back on his head, and made to leave.

"I'll see you out, Sheriff," Lyle said.

"Thank you, Sheriff Flanagan," Peggy said, standing as the men headed toward the front door of the cottage. Her heart had been pounding the entire time the sheriff had interrogated her, but now it began to slow. She would feel even better when Lyle returned.

She had no problem admitting Lyle was her security blanket at this time. When he wasn't with her, she felt afraid. Peggy knew it was foolish to feel this way. Lyle Peterson was as much a stranger to her as the sheriff was, and yet, she trusted him explicitly.

It wasn't long before Lyle returned. "It's only me," he called from the front of the house. Peggy appreciated he didn't want to startle her yet again. He was a gentleman through and through. There were not many like him left anymore. Even at the hospital, male patients tried to grope the nurses despite their illness.

It had got to a point she dreaded going to work. Peggy's thoughts were out of control. She knew they were. This business, these men who murdered her father, had her reeling. Never in her life had she felt so afraid.

The click of the lock reassured her even more. She glanced up as Lyle entered the kitchen, and smiled. Warmth filled her having him near. If only they'd met in better circumstances. Running from killers was no way to meet your soulmate, but Peggy had to admit that's how she now saw Lyle.

Perhaps in a few days all of that would change. They were forced together under extraordinary circumstances, which meant, for Peggy at least, this was not true love. How could it be? No, it was merely a case of having artificial feelings for the man who saved her life.

She watched his every move as Lyle stepped toward her. Her heart fluttered as his arms wrapped her in his warmth. Peggy leaned her head against him and listened to his pounding heart. "I'm here for you," he whispered. In that moment, Peggy knew she wanted to stay like this forever.

Chapter Twelve

Lyle knew he shouldn't be holding her like this. Peggy was not his wife. Heck, she wasn't even a woman he was courting. His actions could lead to her being seen as a tainted woman. It simply wouldn't do.

At this time, no one except the doc and the sheriff knew she was here. Still, there could be consequences. For Peggy at least. His reputation would stay intact – the men in these situations were never labelled the way women were.

What to do about it was the question. The sheriff had suggested they marry. Lyle had been taken aback. It was the last thing he'd expected the man to say. Except the sheriff was right. It would solve more than one problem.

As Sheriff Flanagan had pointed out, having Peggy sleep in the spare room was not exactly safe. If someone did manage to break in, which Lyle knew was highly unlikely but still possible, would he be able to get to her in time? The two bedrooms were not far apart, but in a situation like this, time was of the essence.

Lyle gently lifted Peggy's chin so she was looking up at him. "The sheriff made a suggestion as he was leaving," he said gently. Was he even doing the right thing in telling her?

Her eyes bore into his, silently questioning. When he didn't elaborate, Peggy frowned. "What did he say?" Her blue eyes cut right to his soul, and Lyle couldn't pull his gaze away.

"He said we should…" Lyle paused. He wasn't sure of the reaction his words would have. Lyle took a fortifying breath then let it out slowly. It wasn't such a difficult thing to say, was it? Then why was he so afraid of saying it? "He believes we should get married to protect your reputation." The words came out in a rush. It wasn't the way he'd planned, but there was nothing he could do about it now.

He continued to gaze into her face. Peggy closed her eyes, but only for a moment. She licked her lips, and his heart fluttered. When she opened her mouth to speak, anticipation filled him, but it was her words that sent a thrill down his spine.

"It sounds like a good idea," she whispered, then rested her head against his chest again.

Beyond agreeing to marry, they'd made no plans. Would it be a marriage of convenience, or a real marriage? Lyle had convinced himself many years ago, he would never marry. He was a confirmed bachelor, and had been for as long as he could remember.

What he hadn't grasped was simple – the right woman hadn't come into his life. Now she has.

They stood like that for what seemed a long time. Their arms entwined, their hearts beating as one. Lyle knew he was well past his prime, and yet Peggy didn't even flinch when he'd passed on the sheriff's suggestion.

They were both of a similar age, he was certain. Peggy had a career, which was quite unusual for a woman of her age. Looking after her father all those years – had she sacrificed love for him? It had become clear to Lyle, her father, William Martin had also made sacrifices. In his case, he had risked his principles to save his daughter.

It was something he'd told the sheriff when they were alone. He received a grunt in return. What it meant, Lyle wasn't sure, but it was a moot point as they would likely never know.

"The sheriff is coming back shortly. He said he would bring the preacher." He let his words sink in.

It was a lot to take in, he knew.

"Today?" Peggy sounded shocked. It wasn't hard to understand – everything was happening quickly. He was comfortable with it, since it meant protecting her reputation.

"Is that alright? It's *your* reputation at stake, not mine."

Peggy glanced up at him and smiled. "I don't mind," she whispered. "I would like to tidy up, and perhaps change into something worthy of a marriage ceremony."

She didn't wait for him to answer but pulled out of his arms and headed straight to the bathroom. His eyes followed her until Peggy was out of sight. The strangest thing was, despite being put into a situation where he had little choice, Lyle was not unhappy about marrying Peggy.

Today had been eventful in so many ways, not all of them good. What was about to occur was definitely the highlight of his day. Perhaps even his life.

~*~

It wasn't long before the preacher arrived. He brought his wife with him, to ensure the right number of witnesses. Sheriff Flanagan was there, too.

Instead of starting the ceremony immediately he arrived, Preacher Harold Jones, along with his wife, Mary, spent some time getting to know Peggy. It made him feel good knowing they were ensuring she was happy to go ahead. That she didn't feel forced into something she wasn't comfortable with because of her desperate situation.

His eyes were locked on his beautiful bride. She was quite disheveled when she arrived, but now, Peggy was a picture to behold. When she said she would fix her hair and clean up, he hadn't anticipated the difference it would make. She had also chosen one of his mother's favorite gowns to wear for the ceremony.

Mary Jones brought a lovely bouquet of flowers for Peggy to hold, which was unexpected. The look on his bride's beaming face said more than words ever could.

When the time came for them to stand side by side, Lyle's heart pounded. He imagined Peggy was the same. He reached out and held her hand. His bride was shaking. Whether it was the thought of marrying him, a stranger, or for some other reason, Lyle didn't know.

He was certain she wasn't afraid – not of him, anyway. In a matter of only a few days, not only was her father murdered, but Peggy also had to run for her life. She also had to trust a complete stranger to keep her safe. As if it wasn't enough already, she is pushed into marrying the person who vowed to protect her.

It was little wonder she was trembling. Lyle squeezed her hand, and Peggy glanced up at him. "Thank you," she mouthed, and her face seemed to relax.

It was then Lyle realized he didn't have a wedding ring. "I'm sorry," he whispered to her, then left her side. "I'll be back," he said, as her face contorted. True to his word, Lyle returned moments later. "My mother's wedding ring," he said breathlessly.

The preacher nodded and began the ceremony. "Dearly beloved," he began. The marriage ceremony was over in a short time. No more than ten or fifteen minutes, Lyle guessed. "You may kiss your bride," the preacher said, then glanced at Peggy. "Your choice," he told her, and Lyle expected Peggy to refuse. Instead, she went up on her toes and kissed his lips.

The kiss was chaste and didn't last long, but his lips tingled for what seemed a lifetime afterwards.

Lyle wasn't sure what Peggy expected from this marriage. He didn't know if she even wanted to stay married to him once she was safe again.

His heart shattered at the very thought of losing her. Now he had finally found his soulmate, he did not want to lose her. Not for any reason.

Chapter Thirteen

Peggy was overwhelmed. A lot had happened. Not only in the past few days, but in the past hour as well.

When she arrived at the blacksmith's shop, sneaking past Lyle as he worked, little did she know later that day, they would wed. She wasn't complaining. Lyle was everything she would want in a husband.

He was kind and caring. Not to mention protective of her. He had gone out of his way to ensure her safety and had even given Peggy his mother's clothes to wear. On the other hand, he enjoyed her cooking. It was a small price to pay to see him happy and well-fed.

It was then she realized there was no wedding meal. The pair had already eaten supper, and it was delicious, if she did say so herself.

Peggy shook her head. She was disappointed, but it wasn't like she had time to prepare for their wedding – with only a few minutes notice. It was nothing short of a miracle she'd managed to make herself presentable in the short time available.

Lyle didn't seem at all disappointed, and she decided it was the main thing. Peggy glanced down at the gold band on her finger. It was a treasured family heirloom – his mother's wedding ring. She was surprised he trusted her enough to become the caretaker of his mother's precious jewelry.

"I…I have cake if anyone is interested," Peggy announced a short time after the ceremony ended.

Mary Jones refused the offer. "My dear, Peggy," she said gently. "I wouldn't dream of staying here and ruining your wedding night."

Peggy's face filled with heat. Did Mrs. Jones not know why they'd married? Theirs would not be a real marriage. It was merely a pretense. At least Peggy had assumed it to be the case. What if she was wrong?

What if Lyle had other ideas? Warmth filled her, which shook Peggy to her core. She trusted Lyle with her life, and agreed to marry him, with no conditions imposed. Did that mean theirs *was* to be a real marriage? The kind her parents had until Mother had died.

Peggy had long given up on meeting the man of her dreams. As a teenager, she'd longed to meet the right man for her. The years in between then and now had frozen her heart. Lyle seemed to be the perfect husband. He had managed to thaw her heart, and also managed to make her feel again.

She had become immune to everything around her. Every day was the same – get up and go to work. Go home and prepare meals. Peggy now knew she'd been on the brink of a breakdown but had no way of knowing it before. Looking back, her father was the same. He was no longer happy, and simply went through the motions.

How long had he been killing patients for criminals? Her mind recalled the date of the first murder he'd documented. It was mere days after her mother's death.

Peggy shoved her fist into her mouth as realization hit, and she ran from the room. Her mother hadn't died of natural causes as she'd been told. Those men, they had murdered her mother because Father refused to cooperate. Is that why he'd done as they asked after her death? Had they then threatened Peggy's life?

Father must have been miserable, killing off patients he would normally have fought to save. The revelation made her light-headed and filled her with fear. She now knew those men would stop at nothing to get whatever they wanted.

"Peggy?" Lyle said, entering the spare room where she'd fled. "What is it? What has you so upset?"

She sat on the edge of the bed, tears rolling down her face. Lyle wiped them away. "I apologize," she said, then reach in under the mattress for the journal. Peggy quickly opened it, and her eyes, still brimming with tears, scanned the first entry.

It was all there to see. How she'd missed it before, Peggy wasn't sure. Perhaps it was because she was fighting to get away and save her life. Or it could have been because she was still in shock over her father's murder. Either way, it was all there in his own handwriting.

I've come to the conclusion there is no way out of this predicament. Two equally vile choices have been presented to me – do what they demand, and discreetly kill specific patients for them, or lose another cherished family member. This time, my daughter.

"This can't be true," Peggy said between sobs. "They murdered my mother all those years ago?" She swiped at her eyes, but the flood of tears would not stop. "And now my father. Do you think they know about the journal?" Her heart was ripped to shreds. Peggy could no longer think straight. Lyle sat her back on the edge of the bed.

She stared as he thought about his next words. "It's a possibility," Lyle told her. "We need to hide it where they will never find it."

Did he think they would break in? After all his talk of being safe here, and the cottage being impenetrable? She should have known better – no building, not even the strongest could withstand even the most determined adversary.

"Do you trust me?" Lyle asked gently. "I have what I believe is the safest hiding place here." He studied her then, waiting for an answer.

Except Peggy was confused. Did it mean Lyle didn't want her to know where he was about to hide her father's journal? "Of course I trust you," she whispered. "But this is not your burden to bear." Peggy knew it to be the truth. No matter they were now married, she didn't want to put Lyle in a difficult situation.

The warmth coming from her new husband was comforting. It only added to her confusion. "Are the guests still here?" she asked, finally remembering them. "They must all think the worst of me." Tears pooled in her eyes, and Lyle pulled her into him.

"They have all left. We are here alone," he said. Moments later he stood, pulling Peggy up with him. They moved into the kitchen where Lyle pulled out a paper bag from a drawer. After putting the journal in it, he tied it up with string. "Are you sure you want to know where the journal will be hidden?"

His concern was touching. She'd already put him in an extremely dangerous situation, and didn't want to make things worse. "I'm positive."

Lyle led her out to the blacksmith's shop which was locked and secure. He then headed straight for the wooden box that held the coal he used in the forge.

"No one would think to look here," he said with confidence as he began to unload the coal, placing the journal as far back as possible. He then covered the journal with coal.

No matter how well it was hidden, Peggy was certain her pursuers would set the building alight if they couldn't locate the one thing they had to ensure was eliminated – her father's damning journal.

Chapter Fourteen

Despite being covered in coal dust, and feeling a little worse for wear, Lyle was worried about Peggy.

She now knew the truth – her father had murdered both strangers and acquaintances to ensure her safety. It was a lot to bear.

As he continued to throw coal back into the wooden storage box, Peggy helped. Not that he asked her to, but because she wanted to. Right now, anything to pacify her was worthwhile. She was understandably distraught, and Lyle completely understood why.

William Martin's only other option was to go to the law. According to Peggy, the local sheriff was as dirty as the coal they were handling. Besides, alerting law outside of the town, without the killers knowing, would be tricky.

Despite telephones being invented only a few years ago, it was not readily accessible. Even today, Granville did not have the luxury of the telephony system.

Peggy's father had been placed in an untenable situation. He had no option but to comply with the killer's wishes.

Lyle glanced up at Peggy. Her face was covered in coal dust, which given any other situation would have been cute. Her tears made tracks down her face, proving her absolute grief at the information she had now discovered.

He wanted nothing more than to pull her close and let her pour her heart out. Replenishing the box with the coal was a much more pressing task. Her eyes pleaded with him to hold her, and his heart desperately wanted to comply. He had to complete this task as a matter of urgency.

Who knew what could happen in the next hour? Or even the next few minutes? Time was of the essence in a situation like this.

As he reached for the last two pieces of coal, Peggy had the same idea. With his hands now covering hers, his heart fluttered. Peggy's eyes searched his, and if he didn't know better, Lyle would think she saw right down into his soul.

Never before in his life had his heart overruled his head. Until the moment he met Peggy. Lyle now understood it wasn't only due to her dire circumstances. It was Peggy. There was something about her that appealed to him in ways Lyle had never experienced before.

He knew emphatically, he never would again.

Lyle continued to stare at Peggy, totally and utterly mesmerized. Finally, he lifted his hands, pulling hers away, then threw the last of the coal into the box. He stood then, pulling her up with him.

Despite the situation, despite the coal dust, and the mess they must both be in, he leaned in and kissed Peggy's lips. She didn't flinch or refuse. It was completely the opposite – as he pulled away, she reached out and guided him back to her.

Lyle kissed his bride in a way that was worthy of his new wife. Then he slipped his arms under her and carried Peggy back to the cottage.

~*~

Despite the haste of their unconventional wedding ceremony, Lyle decided their new married life had begun perfectly.

Apart from being covered in coal dust, that was.

He had no pressing tasks that needed attention, so this new day, the first full day of married life, was dedicated to his new bride.

Except Peggy's priorities lay elsewhere. The first thing she wanted to do after waking this morning, was bathe. Not that he disagreed with her, they both needed to clean up far better than the quick wash they had last night.

After having a luxurious breakfast of bacon and eggs, with toasted bread on the side, Peggy cleaned the kitchen. While she cleaned, Lyle ran her bath. If that's all it took to make her happy, it worked for him.

Lyle couldn't remember feeling this satisfied before. He'd lived his life as a single man, and believed it suited him. Now he was married, even if only for a short time, and knew he'd done the right thing. Not only because it would help Peggy, but it felt so right.

He finally understood his parents. They were happy together. Despite the long hours his father had worked in his blacksmith's shop, they led blissful lives. At least through Lyle's eyes.

Never before had Lyle felt at a loss. He simply worked when there was a lull in his day. No matter what time of day or night it was – he would go back to work. The forge was always kept burning, so it was a relatively easy task.

Only now, Lyle understood why his mother would scowl when Father disappeared to work *on one last project*. Her disdain may have only lasted seconds, but it was there each and every time his father announced he would be back soon.

He never was. His father would disappear for hours at a time. Even Lyle tired of it sometimes, despite the man being Lyle's hero. The memory tugged at his heart, and Lyle vowed he would not follow in his father's footsteps. He would be the husband Peggy deserved.

All he had to do now, was ensure he kept his promise.

~*~

Their first day of marriage was a good one, Lyle concluded. Peggy had thoroughly enjoyed her leisurely bath – at least that's what she told him. The lines of stress had all but disappeared from her face, and she seemed more relaxed.

Neither of the two voiced their concern about her safety. Sheriff Flanagan promised to set things in motion, and Lyle had no choice but to believe he would.

Despite believing the sheriff, Lyle was surprised to hear the pounding on the door of the blacksmith's shop. The expression on Peggy's face was one of concern, and Lyle's pounding heart mimicked her concern.

"You stay here," he demanded, then headed toward the sound, pulling on his gun belt as he went. It still felt strange, as Lyle rarely kept a gun at his side, but circumstances demanded it.

"It's Virgil," the voice called through the door. "Sheriff Flanagan," he said when Lyle didn't budge.

Although the pounding had stopped, Lyle's heart continued to pound. With one hand on his gun, Lyle carefully unlocked the large door, opening it only a crack. His relief when he saw it was the sheriff was palpable. "Sheriff," he said, then opened the door wider. "Can't be too careful," he said as way of explanation.

Locking the door behind them, he waved the sheriff into the cottage. Peggy was in the kitchen. Either it was her favorite place to be, cooking up a storm, or this room felt safe to her. He wasn't sure which one it was, but she seemed happiest when she was busy.

"The sheriff is here," Lyle said as they entered the kitchen. He didn't want to startle her.

Peggy spun around to face them. "Ah, just in time, Sheriff," she said. "I have muffins straight out of the oven." Pulling down three mugs, she made coffee for the men without asking, believing neither would refuse. "I'm afraid the muffins are plain," she said. "We need fresh supplies from the mercantile." Her eyes went to Lyle, and he knew that was his cue to top up the pantry supplies.

"Make a list and I'll get whatever you need." It was no problem. Or was it? "On second thought, I can't leave you alone."

"I can stay here while you're gone," Virgil said. "Or I can get your supplies. Either way works."

Why Lyle hadn't thought of such an easy solution, he wasn't sure. His mind was trained on keeping Peggy safe, and nothing more. "Thank you. It's very kind of you." He was beginning to understand Sheriff Virgil Flanagan was not one of the bad guys. He seemed to be doing all he could to keep Peggy safe.

With a mug of hot liquid in front of each person, and a plate of muffins on the table, it felt like three friends sitting around having a casual conversation. Except this was far from casual. Virgil had news, he told them.

"The marshals have got back to me," he said, his words surprising Lyle as he had no idea Virgil was contacting the marshals. Although he wasn't obligated to tell Lyle or Peggy anything. "They have been after this gang for a long time. Years, apparently."

"They know them?" Peggy asked, her voice incredulous. "If they'd stopped them earlier, my parents would both be alive today."

"Both your parents?" the sheriff asked, his surprise evident.

Lyle explained about the journal and the entry they'd discovered last night. "The journal is now well hidden, so you'll have to take our word for it," he said firmly.

Sheriff Flanagan studied him before speaking again. "I don't doubt you for one minute. The gang is known as The Ravagers. They kill anyone who gets in their way."

Peggy gasped, and Lyle covered her hand with his.

"I'm sorry, Peggy," Virgil said. "It's what I was told, but I know little else. Help is on the way, which is the main thing."

Lyle glanced at his new wife who was ghostly white. Not only had she learned her mother was murdered by this gang, but she also now knew they wouldn't stop until they eliminated her as well. "We'll protect you," Lyle told her.

"And you, who will protect you?" she whispered.

Chapter Fifteen

Peggy's hands shook, making it difficult to write a shopping list. She stared at the few supplies on the pantry shelves but saw nothing.

As a nurse, she knew what was happening – she was in shock. It was all too much for her to handle. The men still sat at the kitchen table. They were discussing her situation, which had now become Lyle's situation.

She should never have agreed to marry him. All it had achieved was to put him in danger. "Flour," she whispered, then added it to her list. Peggy didn't even recognize her own writing; her hand shook so much. "Apples, blueberries, sugar…" Her voice didn't sound like her own either.

If she were a patient, she would sit them down and give them a mug of sweet tea. Also, something sweet to eat. If that didn't work, she would lay them down and keep them warm. Except she was a nurse. She didn't need any of those things, simply because she recognized her symptoms.

"Peggy?" Lyle's voice reverberated through her head. It was like she was in an echo chamber. Without warning, she felt as though she was floating through the air. "It will be alright," he whispered in her ear.

Being close to him made her feel safe. It didn't rid her of the shock, only time would do that, but feeling the warmth of his body next to hers, and his arms holding her were all Peggy needed in this moment.

As he lay her down on the bed, then covered her with a blanket, Peggy closed her eyes. Perhaps sleep would rid her of this fear. She soon drifted off to sleep.

~*~

"It's not an easy position to be in," Virgil said.

Although he kept his voice low, Peggy staggered out of the bedroom to hear the conversation. The men were talking about her, and she should be part of it. As though he sensed her presence, Lyle glanced up. "How are you feeling?" he asked as he stood, then stepped over to her side as she entered the kitchen.

Did he think she was an invalid? "I am quite capable of walking by myself," she said gruffly, then regretted her words. "I apologize," she said, then headed toward the stove. "I am feeling much better," she added. Reaching for clean mugs she asked, "What did I miss?" She wouldn't mention her weakness, or the fact Lyle had carried her into the bedroom to ensure she made it there. Doing so would admit her defeat. Peggy promised herself she would be strong, and she intended to keep that promise. It was a pity her body hadn't listened.

While she waited for the kettle to boil, she collected up the soiled dishes. Had the men really sat at the table all this time and talked? What had they discussed? Did she need to know? These questions and more ran through her mind.

"Did you hear that?" Lyle asked the sheriff. "Someone is pounding on the door." He stood then, and fear filled her. Peggy did not like the person she'd become. She had never been afraid. Not of anything. Now it felt as though everything scared her. Except for Lyle. Being by his side was different. He made her feel safe.

As though he'd read her thoughts, he stood beside her. His arms wrapped around her, holding her tightly, he promised she was safe.

With the pounding getting louder and more frequent, the two men left the kitchen. Peggy watched as they went, trying to calm herself. Surely the killers wouldn't pound on the door to secure entry. They were more likely to break the door down. Lyle assured her it was impossible.

Every minute they were gone seemed like an hour. Peggy was far too nervous to do anything and stood helplessly as the kettle boiled. Perhaps she could attempt to write the shopping list again? Peggy knew exactly what she was doing – trying to distract herself.

"We're back," Lyle said as they finally returned. "We have some visitors."

Peggy slowly turned around to face them. If it were the killers, she was certain Lyle, and the sheriff would not have led them to her. Instead, they would fight to the death. The thought of it left her reeling.

"Let me introduce you," Virgil said. "The marshals are," he pointed to each man as he spoke. "Jonas, Rusty, Cody, and Griff."

"Mrs. Peterson," Griff said. "Pleased to meet you. We will get those men, have no doubt."

"It's Peggy, and I hope you do." She had always been blunt and to the point. Peggy had no intention of changing now.

"You better get the shopping list done," Lyle said. "I'm sure the marshals will be hungry."

They didn't object. "Coffee first, then the list," Peggy told him. There were priorities, and she knew what men liked, and it was a mug of hot coffee after a long day of travel. "Please, take a seat," she told them all. "Either in here or the sitting room." The last thing she needed was men hanging around the kitchen. If they sat around the table, fine. But standing and filling the already small space didn't work for her.

Lyle glanced across at her. He opened his mouth to speak then shut it again. She glanced at him curiously. As though she'd given him the go-ahead to say whatever was on his mind, he spoke to Griff. He seemed to be the one in charge. "I noticed two men loitering outside yesterday. I don't know if it was the men you're after."

Virgil answered. "I checked them out after I left here. They were traveling salesmen. They're gone now."

Peggy was relieved. It was one less thing to worry about. Except the men the marshals sought were still out there, somewhere. A shiver went down her spine, and it shook her to the core. "How do we know the men who murdered my parents are not here in town, waiting to pounce?"

"I'm afraid there's no way to tell," Griff told her. "If they are here, we'll find them. Our main objective is to protect you. In the process of doing so, we plan to catch the gang of murderers and see them hanged."

His words gave Peggy some sense of reassurance, but words didn't mean a thing unless actions followed. Father would be grateful, she knew. She didn't blame him for what happened – he was as helpless to do anything, as Peggy felt now. She only wished she'd known the situation. Together they might have been able to see those men put away for the rest of their lives.

Chapter Sixteen

With the small kitchen being crammed with marshals, the noise became almost jarring. Peggy was already distressed, and Lyle wasn't certain she could take much more. Watching her she seemed fine, but he knew better. Even simply pouring boiling water into the mugs, she faltered.

He went to her side. Without a word, he took over the task of making the coffee. Peggy gazed up at him, but didn't say anything. She then added muffins to a plate. Together they served their guests. "Thank you," she whispered when they'd finished. "I don't think I could have done it without you."

Lyle was certain she would have, but it would have posed difficulties. It already had.

With her hands still shaking, he was certain Peggy was overcome as well as concerned. He, too, was anxious. If the marshals were as worried as they'd sounded, and he had no doubt it was true, he should be alarmed.

And he was. One thing he was certain of – no one could break in here. They could not penetrate the blacksmith's shop. It was built to withstand anything.

Except perhaps if they used some kind of explosive device to break through the walls. Lyle doubted it would be the case.

Then again, the men in question seemed determined. If you were the type of people who recruited an upstanding citizen to murder your enemies, one who was unwilling without threat to his family, you would not flinch at going to such lengths.

He didn't care about his property. It was never an issue for Lyle. His loyalty lay firmly with his wife now, and keeping her protected and away from those awful men.

How his life had changed in a little over twenty-four hours. For Peggy, her world had been completely turned upside down. The noise level finally dropped as the four marshals began eating his wife's delicious muffins. She certainly was an excellent cook. "Sit down and rest," he told her. "You need a break." He glanced down into her face. What he saw, worried him.

Lyle lifted his hand and traced the lines around her eyes. His fingers burned a trail down to her lips. Despite their company, and the audience surrounding them, he leaned in and gently kissed her. Peggy sagged against him.

It took only seconds for Lyle to cradle her in his arms. If he could make her feel better, even if it was only for mere minutes, he would take the opportunity.

"These muffins are the best I've ever had," Rusty said. Peggy glanced up at him and smiled.

"Once I have more supplies, I'll do more baking," she said quietly, then rested her head on Lyle's chest again.

The shopping list was long, but necessary. With four extra men to feed, five if they counted the sheriff, Peggy needed far more supplies than Lyle would normally purchase. He was to be accompanied by *one of his friends*, to avoid rumors or suspicion. Arriving during the day, the marshals would surely have been seen entering the blacksmith's shop. This way, Griff said, they could control the narrative, rather than the locals.

It made perfect sense.

Rusty was assigned to go with him, despite Lyle's protests. He didn't need protection; they were here for his wife. "You never know with this gang," Rusty told him. "Their reputation alone tells me they will kill anyone who gets in their way."

Lyle glanced both ways before crossing the road to the mercantile. It was something he always did, but today, he did so with more purpose. Granville was by no means a large town, but it also wasn't small. Travelers came here on a regular basis, and they didn't take the care of locals.

But that wasn't what he was looking for. Today he was keeping his eyes open for anyone who looked out of place. For men who appeared cagey, trying to hide in plain sight. When he glanced at the marshal standing beside him, it was clear Rusty was doing the same. Except in Rusty's case, he didn't know what was normal and what wasn't.

"I don't see anything suspicious," Lyle said matter-of-factly. "What about you?"

Still glancing about, Rusty said, "Not a thing. The place is near deserted."

It was then Lyle realized what had been bothering him. "You're right. I should have noticed. There are normally a few people wandering about, but not tonight."

Suddenly Rusty was on alert. "Let's hurry over to the mercantile and get whatever supplies you need. I have a bad feeling in my gut."

Lyle's hand went to his holster. It hovered there until they were inside and no longer sitting ducks. "Evening, Mary," Lyle said once inside. "This is my friend, Rusty."

"Nice to meet you," Mary said. Except her manner didn't quite match her words.

"Likewise," Rusty answered. He seemed to be on alert, his eyes darting about the store.

It was all very cordial, but Mary didn't seem like her usual jovial self. Apart from appearing stressed, her eyes constantly darted to a blind spot in the store. "I'll take that list." she said and reached out a hand for it.

Never had Lyle seen her like this. Not in all the years he'd lived in Granville, and that was a very long time.

Mary reached for a box from under the counter. She picked up a pencil and wrote something on the base of the box, then flashed it toward the two men. "Man with a gun," she'd written.

Immediately, Rusty flew into action. "Where?" he whispered. Using only one finger, Mary pointed. "Stay here," he told Lyle, but Lyle was having none of it. Who knew what might happen to Rusty if he confronted the man alone?

What happened next was utter chaos. The man kicked, grunted, and even punched. It took both of them to overtake the stranger. It wasn't someone Lyle had seen before.

Even after it was all over, and Rusty had restrained the man, Lyle wasn't sure how it went down. The man cowered in the corner, as though he was afraid of being found. He stood out as being a drifter, from the state of his clothes. The pungent odor that came from him was another sure give away.

At first Lyle was relieved. They'd caught the man. At least in Lyle's mind Peggy was now safe. Except it soon became clear this was a man looking for money to get a meal. He'd tried to rob the mercantile. He was not here to find Peggy.

Still, he was arrested, as he should be. Rusty took the man to the sheriff's office and locked him in a cell. The stranger ended up with the one thing he wanted – a hot meal. There would likely be many more to come.

By the time Rusty arrived back at the store, most of the supplies were in the large box. Mary had calmed down and decided it might be time to hang up her apron. Since her husband, Joseph, had died, she'd run the store alone. With only the two of them there, Mary told Lyle she no longer felt safe.

Lyle really felt for her. He'd long believed her to be brave, continuing to run the store. It was a big task with long hours and hard work. "Perhaps you could get an assistant," he suggested. Food for thought at the very least.

As he walked away carrying the large box, something caught Lyle's eye. "I'll take one of those as well," he said, pointing to the item he craved.

Mary smiled. "This one is on the house. You likely saved my life."

Lyle shook his head. "Even so, it's a gift for someone special. I want to pay. Put it on my account." He watched as Mary reluctantly followed his instructions.

The two men repeated their checks of earlier and glanced up and down the street. Apart from a couple of drunks leaving the hotel, it was quiet. They crossed the road quickly, and Lyle unlocked the door, ensuring they were inside in the shortest time possible.

"Let me take the box," Rusty said. "You'll need your hands free to give Peggy her gift." He raised his eyebrows and grinned.

"If you're sure?" Lyle asked. Rusty continued to grin.

The pair entered the cottage and followed the sound. Only the sheriff and one of the marshals were at the table, along with Peggy. "The others will be sleeping," Rusty said. "We will take shifts of two at a time."

Peggy had her back to them, but Lyle's heart raced seeing her there, and knowing she was safe. He leaned in and kissed her cheek. "These are for you," he said, handing her a box of candy.

Her beaming smile was the only reward he needed. "Ooooh, thank you," Peggy said, her voice full of delight. It was such a simple gesture, but Lyle wanted to show her he cared, but also to make her feel better.

These past days had been a terrible trial for her. Lyle hoped having him in her life would make things better for her.

He knew, however, it couldn't happen until the Ravagers gang were caught and punished for their heinous crimes.

Chapter Seventeen

Peggy stared at the box of candy. It was a lovely gesture on Lyle's part, but what really touched her heart was Lyle thinking about her in this way. She glanced up to see him grinning. Did it mean he was happy to see she loved his gift?

She couldn't help but want to hold him. Few men were willing to show their affections in front of other men, but Lyle was an exception. He had proven it several times already.

As she turned to face him, Peggy stumbled. Lyle was right there to steady her. He seemed to always be there to help when he was needed. She'd always thought it was a joke when she'd heard the term *knight in shining armor*, but it was truly what Lyle had been for her.

He'd held her when she needed it, hidden and protected her when necessary. He'd even married Peggy to maintain her reputation in the process of keeping her safe. He was a good man. Someone she had come to rely on. And what had she given him in return? Little more than some decent meals.

"Sorry," Peggy said, as Lyle's hands held her, ensuring she didn't fall. "Your gift was beautiful." She felt heat rise in her cheeks. Why she felt embarrassed, Peggy wasn't sure. Lyle was her husband, so there was no need to feel that way.

Perhaps it was because they had an audience. She didn't know.

Lyle stared down into her face. "Everything you wanted is in the box." He glanced at the large box now sitting on the kitchen counter. "Mary was very happy to fill this order." He grinned again. It was as though there was some sort of secret between Lyle and Mary, and she guessed there was. The mercantile owner had been making Lyle's meals. For how long, Peggy didn't know.

The fact she'd put in such a large order would have told the mercantile owner he now had someone cooking for him. Did Lyle tell her he was now married? It was unlikely since gossip about his marriage might lead the killers to her.

She hugged Lyle, then stepped away from him to put her new supplies away. It was silly, she knew, but Peggy felt hollow and totally alone without him holding her. The more he held her in his arms, the more she wanted to be held.

Was it always like this for newly married couples? She mentally shook the thought away. They'd only married to protect her reputation. Except, now it had turned into something completely different.

Peggy sorted the supplies and carried them into the pantry. It was getting late. Too late tonight to bake, but she would need to do so in the morning. With all these hungry mouths to feed three times a day, she would be kept quite busy over the next…what? Few days?

She hoped and prayed this nightmare would end soon. Not only for her sake, but for Lyle's. He needed to get back to his normal routine and take back his life.

By the time she'd finished unpacking the supplies and placing them in some sort of order in the pantry, Peggy was ready for bed. She was dog-tired. It had been a big day in many ways, and tomorrow promised to be the same.

If not worse. Peggy would be up with the birds, ready to look after the brave men sent to protect her. She hoped, in the process of protecting her, none were injured or worse. The mere thought of it made her sad.

When she found out about her father's actions, Peggy was angry. She blamed William Martin for his own death. Learning her mother was murdered made her sad, but even more furious at her father.

Until she realized he'd complied to keep Peggy safe. And where did it get him? Nowhere, because in the end, they'd murdered him simply because he chose to lead a quieter life in his old age.

Tears filled her eyes, and Peggy brushed them away. Not only was she exhausted, she was melancholy. It wasn't a good way to be.

When she returned, the kitchen was empty. The men had moved to the sitting room, no doubt with a mug of coffee in hand. The plate of muffins was empty, which sent warmth through her. Peggy enjoyed knowing her efforts made people happy, or at least, filled their bellies.

Tomorrow she could do far more baking, now she had a good supply of ingredients.

Peggy was used to waking to sunlight shining through the window. Although the cottage appeared to be a regular dwelling, and had windows, there was no sunlight. As Lyle had told her, the building was completely enclosed. Why Lyle's father would do such a thing, she couldn't fathom. Unless he was in some sort of danger?

According to Lyle, it had been this way for as long as he could remember, which probably meant it was always like this.

Apart from no sunlight, there was no moonlight, and no waking to the sound of birds starting their day. It was disheartening, but for her situation, it meant Peggy was safe. The building was like a fortress.

She hadn't thought about it previously, but it also meant there was no vegetable garden. You couldn't grow anything without fresh air and sunlight. It was a depressing thought.

Peggy wondered how Lyle had lived here so long without the benefit of a fresh breeze coming through the windows. Or the joy of waking to a beautiful sunrise.

For now, it suited her situation, and she had to get used to it.

She slid out of bed, doing so as quietly as possible. She didn't want to wake Lyle. His life had changed because of her presence, and he needed to sleep. He hadn't stopped since the moment he had found her.

Peggy pulled Lyle's robe around herself. With four strange men in the building, she had to maintain her modesty. Even if only her husband had been here, she would have done the same. With no clothes except those on her back, apart from those belonging to his mother, Peggy had slept in one of Lyle's oversized shirts.

She padded out to the kitchen, turning on a lantern once she was out of the bedroom. It was almost pitch black in the cottage at this time of day. The first thing she did was to stoke the fire.

She filled the almost empty kettle with water. It had been full when she went to bed. No doubt the marshals kept up their intake of coffee. Not that it mattered, except now they'd have to wait for refills.

Peggy went to the pantry and found the ingredients she was looking for. Going through the kitchen cupboards, she kept the noise level as low as possible. The last thing she wanted was to disturb the men from their sleep.

The glow of a lantern could be seen in the direction of the sitting room, and she instinctively knew there would be two marshals in there. She put her head around the door and greeted them. "Good morning," she said quietly. They seemed surprised to see her.

"You're up early," Jonas said.

"My usual time," Peggy responded. "I like to get an early start." Her easy banter surprised Peggy. She spoke as though everything was as it should be. Instead of being at home, rising to the sunrise, the twitter of the birds, and the sound of the rooster welcoming the new day, she was here. Going through the motions of normality.

Peggy's heart thudded. Would her life ever be normal again? Was there any chance of her returning home? To the place killers would have eliminated her if she hadn't outsmarted them?

In her heart, Peggy knew she was destined to stay away forever more. In her mind, she wanted to return to the only place she'd ever known as home.

Chapter Eighteen

Lyle was still getting used to having another body in his bed. He never expected to feel this way about anyone, but he fell hard.

He reached across to pull her closer, as he'd done several times before, but found the bed was not only empty, but stone cold. It made him wonder what time it was. He reluctantly climbed out of bed and pulled on his trousers. Then he went to the one place he was certain to find Peggy. In the kitchen.

As he left the bedroom, the aroma filling the cottage confirmed his suspicions. Whatever she was making was filling the cottage with delicious smells. Entering the kitchen, his bride was standing at the kitchen counter, her back to him. Lyle stepped up to her and put his arms around her, whispering in her ear. "Good morning," he said. "I missed you this morning." He felt her stiffen, but only for mere seconds. He should have announced his presence.

She spun around in his arms and gazed up at him. Instead of castigating him, Peggy gazed up into his face. "Good morning," she said, a smile on her face. Then she went up on her toes and kissed him.

Lyle knew he could easily take this treatment every day for the rest of his life. He also knew he had no right to presume. Even though they had consummated their marriage on the evening of their wedding.

It wasn't something he'd planned, and Lyle was certain Peggy hadn't planned it either. There was something between them and it couldn't be denied. They were perfect for each other, and the chemistry was there. Why would you refuse it?

When the kiss was over, Peggy's eyes drifted to his bare chest. She licked her lips, then briefly kissed him again. "I have far too much to do," she said firmly. "You are a distraction I don't need."

Lyle chuckled. He liked being a distraction. He'd never been one before, not ever. It felt good.

His arms tightened around her, stopping his wife from turning back to whatever she was making. "Don't leave me," he begged, his voice low. Instead of complying, she laughed, then threatened him with her flour covered hands. Lyle's arms dropped to his sides.

He didn't want to let her go, but Lyle knew Peggy had work to do. For his part, the marshals presence had taken over the task he'd put on himself – to keep

Peggy safe. He thought about it for a minute. Maybe less.

Having four marshals here was reassuring, but it didn't mean his work was done. She may not like it, but from this moment forward, he would shadow Peggy. Wherever she went, he would go.

Lyle and his trusty gun.

~*~

It wasn't long before the two marshals made their way to the kitchen. "Something smells good," Cody said. "I don't suppose there's coffee?" He grinned, as Lyle knew he would. It seemed marshals could live on coffee, provided it was hot and strong.

How long they would be here, was anyone's guess. Lyle only hoped they found the killers sooner than later. He wasn't sure how much more Peggy could take. Outwardly, she seemed fine. It was as though nothing untoward had happened in her life. Anyone who didn't know better could think she was on a short break. Having a holiday with a friend.

It was far from that.

Lyle's eyes strayed to the kettle. The water was almost boiling. "It looks like you're in luck," he told Cody, and reached for his mug. Peggy's eyes followed his every move. Did she think he was trying to take over her job? What he was doing was meant to help her.

She had her hands in a bowl filled with a dough of some sort. No matter how long he stared at it, Lyle still had no idea what she was making.

"It's bread dough," she said. "For later."

He stood next to Peggy and filled Cody's mug with coffee. The kitchen was small. It was never meant for more than one person preparing meals, or beverages. With the two of them squeezed in side-by-side, Lyle's heart fluttered. He didn't want to move away. He would be happy standing here next to Peggy for the foreseeable future. Not only hours, but years. Decades even. His heartrate quickened.

Lyle had finally admitted to himself he never wanted their marriage to end. Except Peggy might not agree, and that would shatter him. He placed the coffee on the table in front of Cody, then went back to his wife. He held her in his arms and stared down into her face. Her blue eyes were striking and mesmerized him. Lyle wasn't sure he had the courage to say the words but decided to say them anyway. "I…I love you, Peggy," he whispered, keeping his voice low. It was a private moment, and he wanted to keep it that way.

Peggy lifted a hand and pushed back a loose tendril of hair. "I love you, too," she said, but instead of being happy, she was frowning. "What…what is that noise?" she asked, her voice proving her concern.

Lyle listened. The sound was unfamiliar.

Cody stood, then headed for the sitting room. Lyle held Peggy tight. "Everything will be alright," he whispered.

She glanced up at him. "I don't believe it to be the case," she said quietly. "Those men, those murderers, are trying to get inside the fortress your father built to protect his family." Her voice held contempt. Whether it was for Lyle or the killers, he wasn't sure.

What he did know was he would protect her with his life.

Glancing out of the kitchen window, he held a lantern. Lyle stared at the solid wooden wall his father built all those years ago. It may not be visible to strangers, but Lyle could see where the killers were trying to enter the property.

Without further thought, he guided Peggy into the sitting room. One marshal remained. Where the others were, he had no idea.

"I can tell you exactly where they are attempting to get in," Lyle said, his voice breaking. If he lost Peggy, he would have no reason to live. "You protect my wife, and I'll show the others where those men are located."

Cody stared at him in disbelief. "Sounds like a plan," he finally said.

~*~

The three remaining marshals, along with Lyle, went out the front, and onto the street. Lyle locked the door behind them. They broke off into pairs, with each pair going in a different direction. They crept along the perimeter of the property, keeping as close to the wall as they could. Lyle was with Griff, who seemed to be in charge. "They are close to the middle of the wall at the back," he said.

At first, Griff thought it might simply be a distraction. "Most criminals and killers are fools," he said, and these men were proving the theory. The group continued to move slowly and cautiously until they were close enough to see the silhouette of two men. In the limited light from the still rising sun, the other marshals waited for a signal from Griff.

Then, all at the same time, they attacked. Four against two was a good outcome, but they knew the criminal's reactions were unpredictable. Coming from both sides did eliminate some of the danger, and thankfully, between them the men were overtaken without too much resistance.

If these were the only criminals involved, Peggy was now safe. Should there be others lurking about, nothing much had changed.

The two men were arrested and escorted to the sheriff's office, where they were locked up. Hopefully for the remainder of their lives.

If not, Peggy would not be safe. Not ever. It would be an absolute tragedy.

Chapter Nineteen

Peggy was given no choice and was ordered to stay here in the cottage with Cody. She knew it was for her own safety, but sitting here, twiddling her thumbs when she could be doing something? It really irked her.

"I wonder what's happening," she said to Cody.

He studied her. "No idea, but we have no choice but to wait," he said. "This job teaches patience, even in stressful situations like this."

He didn't appear stressed. In fact, Cody appeared downright relaxed. Which was more than she could say for herself. "I might as well get back to my baking," she announced.

Cody scowled. "Not happening," he said, which made her furious. Who did this man think he was bossing her around? "It's for your safety," he added.

"They can't see me. The wall is solid wood," she growled.

It didn't take him even a heartbeat to answer. "Lyle could see where they were trying to get through, so it can't be as solid as he thought it to be."

Shrugging her shoulders, Peggy supposed Cody was right. Baking could wait. Not that she'd been given any choice. Lately it seemed her life was being overrun by men who were trying to manipulate her. It didn't sit well with Peggy.

All her adult life she'd been independent. She alone, made the decision to go to the School of Nursing Excellence in Helena, and earn her qualifications. She'd seen the good work her father had undertaken for many years, and it inspired her.

Little did she know about the horrific things her father had done. About the people he'd murdered. It made her wonder if he fretted over the deaths of those men. Or had he taken the stance that murdering criminals could be justified?

Peggy knew better, and she was certain her father did, too. A niggling thought had her questioning if he'd even thought about the task in that way. "He was forced, you know," she said. Then slapped a hand over her mouth. Lyle suggested they keep the existence of the journal and its location secret for now. With good reason.

Her words, no matter short, and with little basis, surely indicated to the marshal her father's journal, or at least some form of proof, existed.

The way he looked at her now scared Peggy. Was this marshal part of the gang? Surely all four marshals couldn't be tainted. Her heart pounded. Cody stood.

"Where is it?" he asked gruffly as he moved toward her. "You obviously have proof."

The way he stood over her, the way he'd said the words, and his entire demeanor terrified Peggy. "What...what are you talking about?" she spluttered.

It was then Cody showed his true personality. His hand hovered over his holster. His feet apart, and his hands fisted. "It's clear your father kept a record. Where is it?" he asked with far more vigor than Peggy expected from a marshal who was there to protect her. Instead, he was trying to bully her into handing over vital evidence.

"I...I put it under the mattress in the spare room," she said. It wasn't really a lie, since she'd originally put it there. That it was no longer there was beside the point.

Cody stared at her for a heartbeat, then hurried into the spare bedroom. Peggy took the opportunity to run. She didn't get far before Cody caught up with her, and grabbing her by the hair, pulled Peggy to the ground.

Before she knew what was happening, he was sitting on top of her, his hands around her throat. "Where it is?" he ground out, as his grip on her throat tightened.

If he murdered her as a result of her resistance, so be it. Peggy had no intention of handing the journal over to him. Besides, if he killed her, he would never find the journal. It was the one thing that would put Cody and all his criminal friends in jail. Or better still, would see them hanged.

Peggy gasped for air. His hands tightened even more. She saw stars and heard a roaring sound in her head. Confusion set in, and she could feel herself going down a deep dark hole. There was no more fight left in her. At least he couldn't get his hands on the journal.

It was then the entire world went black.

Chapter Twenty

"Get your hands off my wife!" Lyle yelled as he ran at Cody. He reached out and picked Cody up as though he was a ragdoll. Lyle threw the man across the room. He didn't look to see if he was alive or dead.

Cody gasped hearing Lyle's voice, and he dropped his hands. "I…wasn't trying to hurt her," he said. "Someone broke in, and…"

"Liar!" Lyle yelled as he kneeled down next to Peggy. His heart broke seeing her lifeless body. He pulled his gun from its holster, and now pointed it at this murderer who called himself a marshal.

Griff hurried over to Cody. "Get your hands in the air," he demanded. Griff sounded calm, unlike Lyle.

He had no time for Cody. Peggy needed him. Her face was red and swollen and she wasn't moving. Bruises were already appearing on her neck.

It hadn't even entered his mind that Cody, or any of the marshals could be dirty. If he'd had even an inkling of the man's intent, he would have stayed with her.

Her death was on him.

His heart was shattered. Lyle put his hand to her wrist. "She's still alive. Barely, but she *is* alive." His words did not reassure him at all, and Lyle picked Peggy up and ran to the doctor's office. If there were murderers still out there, and they killed him trying to save her life, so be it.

Without Peggy, his life was not worth living. He glanced down into her face. Her bright red features terrified him. Her delicate neck was viciously bruised and cut, and the handprints of her would-be killer were clear for all to see.

The moment he arrived at his destination, Lyle pounded on the door. He shouted for the doc to hurry. His relief was palpable when the door finally opened. "In here," Doc said, pointing to the closest consultation room. "What happened?" he asked as he examined his patient.

"She was strangled," Lyle said, his voice breaking. He'd hoped by some miracle she would be revived by the time he arrived at the doc's office. But it wasn't to be. "Not by me!" he explained when the doctor stared at him.

Doc Huggins nodded then performed mouth to mouth resuscitation. Then he did heart compressions. He checked her pulse. "Better, but not strong," he said, then repeated the actions until Peggy's eyes fluttered open.

She appeared to stare unseeing. Lyle's heart shattered. "Give her a minute or two," the doc said, as he stood by her.

Without warning, Peggy spoke. "Where am I? What happened?" she asked, her voice croaky and full of confusion.

"Cody tried to kill you," Lyle said quietly. "Do you remember why?"

She glanced at him, and Lyle saw the relief on her face the moment she recognized him. Peggy reached for his hand. He held her hand tighter than he'd ever done before. He had no intention of letting go any time soon.

"Tell me he didn't get the journal," Peggy croaked.

Lyle glanced at the doc. Why was her voice so raspy? "That's why he tried to kill you? For the journal?" He shook his head. "As far as I'm aware, he didn't get the journal," he reassured her.

In the beginning, Lyle was concerned about the Granville sheriff. Thankfully, he'd been proven wrong. Why he didn't realize Cody was part of the notorious gang, he didn't know. Lyle had always been a good judge of character.

When he thought about it, Cody had been eager to appear normal, except he was always making himself the center of attention. Did he think it made him appear willing to do the best job possible?

The worst part was it worked. Lyle didn't suspect him, and neither did Griff or either of the other marshals. It made Lyle wonder how long he'd been part of the gang. It was no wonder he was happy to stay with Peggy.

As he glanced down into her face, some of the redness had subsided. It was a relief to see her awake and talking, even if her voice was affected.

"I want to keep Peggy here for the night," Doc Huggins said. "Just in case."

Lyle stared at him for long moments. "Then I'll be here, too. I'm not leaving her alone again."

Doc patted his shoulder. "Of course. The chair over there is comfortable enough, although I admit I've never slept in it," Doc said. "I'll get you a cup of tea," he told Peggy. "It will help with the husky throat. It's very common in choking victims," he said reassuringly, then left the room.

Doc soon returned with tea for Peggy, and coffee for Lyle. He left the room again and returned with some blankets. "I'll check in throughout the night. First, I'll stoke the fire, then leave you to it," he whispered, not wanting to disturb his patient who now slept soundly.

"Thanks, Doc. I can fix the fire. I appreciate all you've done for my wife." Lyle glanced across at Peggy sound asleep on the examination bed. He listened carefully to her breathing, to reassure himself she was still alive. Which she was.

He couldn't bear to lose her, now that he'd finally found his soulmate. He loved her dearly. Lyle stared down into her face. Tears came to his eyes at the very thought of not having her in his life.

~*~

With the trial over, things could now get back to normal.

Peggy's relief was clear when the judge found all three men guilty of murder. They were charged with the murders of both her parents, as well as all the people listed in the journal.

Cody was also charged with the attempted murder of Peggy. Not that it made a difference, they were all sentenced to hang a week later in Helena.

Peggy told Lyle she was thankful they wouldn't be hanged in Granville. As much as she'd had some awful experiences here, she also had happy memories, and those were the ones she wanted to remember.

She was making this place her home, much to Lyle's relief, and didn't want her memories of the place further tainted by the memory of the hangings being local.

According to the judge, and backed up by the marshals on the case, Cody was the reason they hadn't been able to locate the gang. He had quite clearly been feeding information to them, keeping them informed of the latest information available. It was his ill-gained information that let them avoid the heavy hand of the law for so long.

What was unclear, was how many murders Cody had personally performed. He'd not so much as flinched at his attempt to kill Peggy, and the judge concluded he was an active participant in all the killings.

Whether it was feasible or not, Lyle didn't care. He was pleased to see those men out of circulation where they could not continue their killing sprees.

Besides, who was he to disagree with the learned judge? The journal had been provided to Griff, who put it forward as evidence at the trial. It was a pivotal piece of evidence.

Peggy said she was relieved to finally be rid of the journal that almost took her life. Lyle was happy knowing she was no longer in danger, and they could begin their new lives together.

Epilogue

Fifteen months later…

Lyle woke to the sun shining through the window. The sound of birds was like music to his ears. It had taken a lot of convincing, but Peggy had finally persuaded him to leave their small cottage in town.

Gone was the fortress his father had built around the blacksmith's shop and their home. Now only the blacksmith's shop was enclosed. The original cottage held far too many bad memories for both of them, and they had decided to make a clean break.

As a result, Lyle sold the business. It allowed him to spend more time with his family.

It was pure luck this small property where they now lived, was available for purchase. It was big enough their children would have a wonderful upbringing with fresh air and natural light, but small enough it wasn't a lot of work.

Lyle employed men to do the heavy work necessary for a busy farm.

He reached out an arm and gently held Peggy as she slept. Her swollen belly was moving. This baby was far more active than their firstborn, William, named after Peggy's father. It was then he heard the cry of his one-year-old son.

Moving quietly so as not to wake Peggy, he went to William's room and lifted the boy from his crib. Lyle changed his diaper and carried him outside to watch the sunrise. It was something he'd always longed to do, but until they moved here, didn't have the opportunity.

Peggy had changed his life in so many ways, and Lyle was thankful to have met her. He stared down into his son's face and saw his mother there. His son would grow up loved and wanted and would always be a beacon for their love.

He pulled the blanket up around William and pointed out the beauty of the sunrise as he'd done many times before. He turned at the sound of movement behind him – Peggy was awake.

She joined them on the porch, a shawl around her shoulders. "It's a beautiful morning," she whispered.

"Indeed, it is," Lyle said as he reached for his wife. He pulled her close, and the three hugged. In a few more months they would be four. Who knew how big their family would expand? Lyle loved his life now he had found his soulmate, and they enjoyed their time together.

Who knew what the future would bring? Provided he had his wife, and his little family, that's all that mattered.

From the Author

Thank you so much for reading my book – I hope you enjoyed it.

I would greatly appreciate you leaving a review where you purchased, even if it is only a one-liner. It helps to have my books more visible!

About the Author

Multi-published, award-winning and bestselling author Cheryl Wright, former secretary, debt collector, account manager, writing coach, and shopping tour hostess, loves reading.

She writes historical romantic suspense and historical western romance.

She lives in Melbourne, Australia, and is married with two adult children and has six grandchildren, and twin great-grandchildren.

When she's not writing, she can be found in her craft room making greeting cards.

Links

Website: *http://www.cheryl-wright.com/*

Facebook Reader Group:
https://www.facebook.com/groups/cherylwrightauthor/

Join My Newsletter:

https://cheryl-wright.com/newsletter/
(and receive a free book)

9 781763 688995